Along The Dotted Line

A (Probably)

-Mostly-

Fiction Novel

by: Passiflora incarnata

Along The Dotted Line

A (Probably)-Mostly- Fiction Novel

By: Passiflora incarnata

ISBN:979-8-218-48631-0

A Note From The Author

To New Readers:

I'm sorry, and you're welcome? This novel absolutely can and does stand on its own. I have included any relevant info in the introductory "fact" section.

However, if after reading, you are curious about the real-life experience that inspired this novel and my interest in incredibly dark shit- please feel free to check out my 5 other titles (all of which are NON-FICTION, but equally odd), most notably the one referenced below, "Post-Hypnotic".

Also, the absence of page numbers is an intentional choice, and a bit of a signature in all of my novels. I feel it helps the reader get "lost" in the story a bit more.

Lastly, the terms "Psychopath" and "Sociopath" will come up multiple times throughout this book. I am not a licensed Psychotherapist or anything remotely close. However- I assure you- I am not being hyperbolic; if anything I am cursed with downplaying horror, usually to my own detriment. I believe words are very powerful and very important. I don't take lightly the ones I chose to utilize. Though I have done my own research out of morbid curiosity, I haven't just read about "monsters" in books and discussed them in seminars- I've actually lived with them. If you're curious or doubtful, see notes on earlier novels.

To Readers Of My Past Novels:

Technically, this (mostly) fiction novel builds on the base of my last (NONFICTION) novel "Post-Hypnotic". Some people may think it odd or unadvisable to write a fictitious follow up or "ending" to a nonfiction work, but I suppose perhaps I wanted to give a bit of "closure" to my readers and to a lesser extent, to myself.

I decided fiction was the best route to avoid the potential issues arising in publishing another strictly nonfiction novel for several reasons. These reasons I allude to (possibly) being: maybe I want a few damn secrets for myself at this point , and some things are a bit unadvisable to publish as fact - even if they are.

I'll leave it at that (see lengthy disclaimer below).

So, I have instead created a lovely, satisfying, fun, dark , thought provoking, little experimental work of (somewhat) fiction which both incorporates some elaborated fact and provides both a satisfying (though (mostly) fictional) conclusion to my previously published, rather dark, strictly nonfiction book "Post-Hypnotic".

Also, the horrifying real experience I detailed in Post-Hypnotic and the research it has spurred just makes for wayyy too good of a spring board for creative exploration as a form of coping and, well, I guess I just couldn't resist.

Enjoy!

The Compulsorily (Lengthy) Disclaimer:

This (mostly) fictional novel builds on the completely true and factual events and experiences outlined in a previously published non-fiction novel entitled "Post-Hypnotic". In addition, this book includes a few colorful, true experiences and research projects thereafter mixed with a healthy dose of creative fiction.

This novel is meant to create a (mostly, probably mostly) fictional, "imaginatively satisfying" continued story and ending of sorts to the true experiences outlined in the aforementioned novel. Also, it is meant to explore potential answers to some lingering questions in a fun and explorative manner.

This is all for the purpose of catharsis, creative expression, entertainment and maybe toying with "the line" between fiction and fact in an experimentally creative conceptual manner - as well as the purposes outlined further down in this lengthy disclaimer.

That being said, as it is my first and only (probably, mostly?) Fictional novel, it is also written to stand on its own. So, though a few seemingly familiar (as well as some [mostly] identical) "characters" may "pop up" to greet long-time readers along the way , they are given different pseudo names than they were in previous (actually completely) non-fiction novels in order to paint the distinction- even

if in a very grey stroke of paint- between a
(mostly) fictional character in this novel , and
the real human (or sociopath, psychopath,
predator etc.) said character is loosely
inspired by... some of whom may have appeared in
earlier (non-fiction) novels as their actual
(non-fictional) selves.

Also, while we're at it:

All names of people (and psychopathic predators
etc.) Have been changed to (mostly) protect the
innocent- and (mostly) innocent- from death
(probably), stalking (mostly) or general legal
or interpersonal unpleasantness. Along similar
lines of thinking, names of business and
organizations have (probably? Well, mostly...)
been (slightly) altered. Names of cities and
states and the like have (possibly?) Been changed
also, but who knows.

That being said, in the (totally crazy)
hypothetical where some (or all) of said
(mostly) re-named "fictional" organizations and
associated individuals are (in fact, actually)
real- I would gamble that there's (perhaps) a
chance that a motivated reader could deduce their
true names with some effort, the internet and a
VPN. In such a hypothetical situation, the
novel, its author and their constituents are in
no way liable for such activities or outcomes.

Much like those streets that have a solid line
on one side of their center and a dotted on the
other, I (like most writers) utilize fact in my
fiction with reckless abandon and without

feeling the need to specify where one begins and the other ends.

However, I will never allow fiction to cross lanes over into what I label "fact".

With these concepts in mind, I have separated the no pass lane- the purely fact -and labeled it as such. After which, you will find a section (the rest of the book), labeled "faction" to denote my (partially) fiction lane , where fact will (often) cross over with no warning or notice.

Lastly and primarily,

This novel is meant to foster a sense of small-scale, social self-policing within and across sometimes isolated and insulating subcultures and communities who all too often bear the brunt of predation by sadistic, soulless, psychopathic, sexual offenders.

That being said, let the record show, this novel and its constituents (officially) in no way support or encourage violence of any kind (outside of what is absolutely necessary in a purely self-defense situation-obviously).

Please play nice folks and don't stalk, assault or murder people (or, sigh, psychopaths etc.) It's not worth the jail time- it's just not. There are so many other creative fun alternatives to enact change and "vengeance" (justice) that make a much bigger impact and won't wreck your life ☺ .

Ok, for real, last one:

As this book is (probably) still (somewhat) based on (some) true events mixed with (likely) a lot of fictitious creative writing and (mostly) surmising / questionable but (somewhat?) educated guesses-

I have to say this... hopefully this is (probably?) (mostly) obvious to you guys, but given the above, I apparently have to make sure I'm incredibly clear: no (obviously), no humans or psychopaths etc. Or any other lifeforms were physically harmed by, or for, or in the process of making this novel or by its author, directly or indirectly- ever.

A Linear Theme:

This novel is meant to make you THINK, maybe even
DIG-

It's meant to make you QUESTION, what you think you
know, what you've been told -

what you haven't, and WHY.

It is meant to encourage a unique, edgy,
uncomfortably meta, paradigm shifting, interactive
experience, not often found in a novel.

Ok, well all that- sure- (maybe?) but the bottom line
is...

this book is really about,

well, lines.

The lines between; brilliance and madness, terror and
exhilaration, love and hate, possession and
protection, fascination and fixation, passion and
obsession, pain and pleasure, vengeance and
bloodlust, the anti-hero and the supervillain...

The line between learning from trauma- from
experience- and letting it blind you to anything
else...

the line between sharpened intuition and trauma
induced hypervigilance, the line between focusing on
the positive and being willfully, callously ignorant
of the suffering.

This book is about the thin blue lines,

the dotted white passing lines, the double yellow DO
NOT PASS lines,

The blurry lines, the curvy lines, the gray and
barely there lines-

Oh, and those pesky line break ones-

That seem to

                keep

  jumping down

            the page,

with every space you advance

            closer to where

  you thought

            "the line",

                        was.

We humans are pretty damn obsessed- err "fascinated"
- with lines;

be warned, this book will perhaps color a bit
outside of some you may(currently) think that you
have.

How Did We Get Here?

There was a light mist not so much "falling" as just overlaying, everything- "How seasonally appropriate", I thought to myself, not that this night needed any help in the "spooky" department. I stood, frantically shaving my "Big Sur" bumper sticker off of the back window of my bright green compact -

not that being sans-bumper sticker alone would suddenly make the jeeringly colorful car disappear into the masses of drab, beige ones surrounding it.

I used the sleeves of my long, black, wool sweater to wipe away the remnants of said sticker- in between wiping my incessantly running nose- and true to the paranoia I felt, checking to be sure that I was still alone on the back street. I shook my head to myself as I began to tape off the windows with cardboard from the alley and tried not to flinch at the sound of the duct tape that I used to secure it.

"How did we get here again?!" I loudly questioned in my own mind with a helpless laugh, as I brought the can of black spray paint up with a still trembling hand, guarded my nose with that same wool sweater, and began to coat the back side of the car first.

How did we get here... and where is "here" exactly?

Well, literally speaking, "here" is a back alley in Oakland, in the middle of the night. Here is me hoping I'm alone, spray painting my compact and securing a (not quite technically legal) alternative tag procured (perhaps) with some assistance by the only person in town who I think I can finally (completely) trust- all in the hopes I won't be recognized ever again.

This is the same reason that my hair is lopped off in an emo sweep wanna be fashion (desperate times desperate measures, latta da da), and soaked in black dye instead of its former crimson glory. Oh, and it's also why I'm wearing blue contacts, despite my irrational (?) fear of putting glass on my eyeballs.

But I digress,

"here"- is me about to attempt to disappear, because- frankly- I don't know what other choice I have left after what I've done...

that and (mostly) what I've fucked with and attempted to expose that THEY'VE done,

that they're doing.

I thought I could stop them, bring them down, but there's just too many people- if you can call them that- involved.

And now,

it's time to run.

But to fully explain where "here" really is, where I am, what the hell is going on and what has me so on edge?

Well, I'd have to start at the beginning, I guess.

Spark

(FACT):

How did I get mixed up in all this shit to begin
with? I'm just lucky like that I guess.

After successfully leaving a deadbeat, violent, live-
in boyfriend who was also a particularly unpleasant
brand of sadist, I found myself re-establishing my
identity- sexually and otherwise- in a beachside
SoCal town. I had integrated into a blues dancing
community to meet new people and was introduced to
both scores of them as well as an even more niche
dance scene called "fusion". What I wasn't
immediately expecting, however, was that the vast
majority of my new "friends" were thirsty poly
couples - several of them active in the social BDSM
scene- hunting for their next unicorn. I also wasn't
expecting them to introduce me to a friend of theirs
who would change my life, forever.

The backdrop to the "tramedy" that ensued was,
naturally, a global pandemic- because why not make
surviving (spoiler alert) the upcoming assault with
a particularly unusual twist feel a little more
isolating than usual, eh?

Despite my initial conflicting mix of instinctual
skepticism and irritating interest in this mutual
friend- this creature- and his growingly obvious
predatory notice of me (first publicly at events and
later publicly online thru the book of faces), we had
never hung out.

In fact, we had never even exchanged DM or texted, we
hadn't exchanged numbers, and we had never even liked
each other's posts. Adding him in the first place

was actually merely a mix of admittedly some curiosity, hesitant interest even, and a social formality as acquaintances in the dance scene.

Then, at the height of Covid and around the time I discovered via the friends (minus the r) who introduced us, that there was indeed a very real cross over between this niche dance circle and both the poly and social BDSM scene, I got a comment from him on a picture of some art I'd posted online.

What followed was basically him getting himself an invite to my apartment under the guise of an afternoon painting sesh- that turned out to be an evening of losing my sense of time and space while being violated in new and (somehow) worse ways than I had already experienced. I could go on, but as this is more of a " post- post hypnotic " story - I'll stick to what's immediately relevant to my "now" . This unpleasant hypnofuck- well, we could call him Dohn Dreeman , or Den Dnby, but for the purpose of this story he'll be referred to as simply "Fuckface".

Fuckface started out his torture with a "question game ", initiated very appropriately with (unbeknownst to me) a quote from a horror movie: "Would you like to play a game ?"

Original, I know.

As my senses faded in terms of control, he utilized a variety of techniques - now nauseatingly obvious- from the NLP playbook and Erickson style hypnosis tactics, while making me keep my eyes closed during the assault that followed. I was technically awake for the whole thing but utterly incapable of stopping it. He made me shower after and made sure to leave zero evidence other than taking a "trophy" via ripping the literal heart off one of my oldest

paintings. I was a shell of myself for weeks trying
to figure out what the fuck happened to me, why I
felt so dead inside, trying to mend the scattered
pieces of my memories from that evening- those 7
hours he had me captive in my own mind.

Worse, I kept finding the door unlocked, kept hearing
footsteps outside my door at odd hours, feeling
"off", foggy headed.

It was HELL.

_____

FAETION:

Soon I'd find that he hadn't stopped with that
night, that he'd also sold me out to his fleet of
sickos via broadcasting the assault to the whole
fucking underworld. That is, until one of said
sickos decided to test his luck and do not only what
the O.G. jack ass did to me but pretend to be my
friend too. That's when the true extent of what had
happened started to take shape in my subconscious...
in my intuition.

It took months, but I put the pieces together. I
found out they worked together in the film industry,
and I confronted my "friend". He made it apparent
that he was fully aware of what had occurred and
also kept alluding to a video.

The latter was especially nauseating as I did have a faint memory of our mutual "friend" pulling out a camera of some kind during that night from hell. Also, as he was an amateur horror film maker, it wasn't exactly a total shock that he'd be the type to take a virtual "trophy".

This Judas character proceeded to attempt a sloppier version of what I'd already been subjected to, but thankfully the combo of my increased knowledge and his subpar prowess left (slightly) less of a scar. I lived thru the night, but as soon as he left my apartment, I started packing. Within the week, I'd fled the city.

Despite my attempts at forgetting- my attempts at drowning out the horror with booze and meaningless sex with strangers- the memories only grew clearer and the rage?

It was seething, pulsating stronger and stronger with every passing day... with every new detail that emerged.

Thanks to the alluded to video and its apparent "use" for additional hypnofucks like my "friend" Judas, it started to become clear that I hadn't really escaped after all. It seemed I was instead, ripe for the hunting. I decided if I wanted to live as myself, have anything close to a "normal life", my options were: give up and kill myself, run or fight these fuckers.

After some considerable deliberation, I decided on a combination of the latter 2 choices.

So run I did.

First to the Central Coast, then to the Sierras and beyond. I moved every few months, changed my hair

color and aliases and phone number and online
accounts every damn time.

At first, I really did feel hunted.

But then,

I STARTED HUNTING.

Kindle

It took time, but eventually, with a lot of effort, I got pretty savvy. I taught myself to hack, code- Linux, Python, OSINT -the whole shebang.

Starting out on this trauma and fury fueled little research project, I thought I was strictly hunting a small group of sick fucks who liked to rape women using hypnosis tactics and NLP techniques and share their "footage" on discord or maybe some dark web server. Slowly though, I began to realize that it was closer to a HUGE subculture of in person and online groups of these sick fucks raping women with their mind games and sharing pics and videos of their crimes as "trophies".

But gradually, as I continued down the deranged rabbit hole I'd fallen into, I accidently stumbled upon something even more sinister- the connection between a handful of these sick hypnofucks who were active within the (otherwise lovely) BDSM world and a real-life cult... well, maybe a *couple* of real-life cults.

The most notable of said cults was an exclusive secret society of extremist sadists, a group I'd only heard whispers of on the fringes of the internet.

"The International Council of Masters", not a group many people have heard of perhaps- but one that's still thriving in the seedy waters of the underworld and flowing through the filthiest corners of the dark web. They are incredibly secretive, so much so, that there's little to no actual information - even referentially - to them on the clear net. What are they exactly? Well, a secret society, a cult really, made up of extremist sadists. They utilize torture, rape, hypnosis and imprisonment -all with a very ritualized flavor. It's said the members wear purple capes in their rituals, and their victims wear white ones. There is one serial killer (apparently labeled "the internet's first serial killer", among other things) who openly claimed to be a member. He (thankfully) ended up on death row.

The only other person I've found who openly claims to be a member is an unidentified "Dom" (read : "master") who I came across via a bit of research on a very popular BDSM dating and hookup site (research I obviously did by way of a shell account made with a VPN and a burner email and cell.) This unnamed "Dom" claimed to be a slaveowner of two females and a member of The International Council Of Masters, and also apparently seeking new additions to his "collection", as well as you know, "fun dates" also.

I've found some indications this squalid little group was alive and popping during the peak of the surrealist movement- which sort of makes sense as Marquis de Sade (the so-called father of sadism) was profoundly instrumental in inspiring the surrealists.

One odd comment that stuck with me from the 7 hours Fuckface was tormenting me, was his mention of surrealism. His love of "surrealist films" and the surrealist movement. Up until that afternoon from hell, I only knew of "Surrealism" in the context of painting , and had no idea there was a whole movement and ideology behind it.

The Surrealist movement was born during the 1920s, and in addition to Marquis De Sade, was largely inspired by Freudian and Marxist ideas. The Surrealists movement's founder, Andre Breton studied medicine for roughly 7 years, but his true passion was psychology.

From its start, the surrealists were fascinated by the unconscious mind, and utilized hypnosis as well as what they called "psychological automatism" (basically involuntary happenings/ dreams/ things your conscious mind isn't in control of... like hypnotic states).

It's rumored that the man responsible for the infamous Black Daliah murder was himself both a physician and a surrealist - who was actively engaging in rape, hypnosis and human trafficking as well as incest.

Personally, I also believe he could have been a member of the I. C. O.M., but who knows, right? Because isn't life just a big, fluffy bundle of wonder?

Also - an interesting (possibly) coincidence? Some sources say that the other cult I mentioned with ties to the BDSM world (more on that later) got its original start in 1921, in London as well.

That latter cult , was something a friend of Fuckface had alluded to.

Regardless of what depths of dark history I.C.O.M. sprung from or what depraved corner of hells fire it got its "inspiration" from, I was sure if it was indeed alive and thriving, it existed - functionally- at the intersection of the covert hypnosis community and the BDSM world.

Given all of the above combined with Fuckface's additional brief allusion to his knowledge of "sexual psychology", claims of his being a "fixture" in certain public BDSM related groups and what seemed like a disturbing level of planning and targeting in his attack on me - I had to wonder... did he have ties to any of this?

I wasn't sure , but I knew I had to learn more.

Conveniently (?) I'd found myself smack dab in the cross hairs of perhaps the most booming area in the country for both BDSM and NLP- as Santa Cruz is the birthplace of NLP and the Bay is the national mecca for the public BDSM scene.

It would seem, I'd also found myself closer than I first imagined possible to some major players at be in both these "taboo" subcultures. The former was a legitimate - albeit scarring- coincidence; the latter, well, I might have helped along, just a wee little bit.

The asinine little Fuckface who started my lovely downward spiral into dark shit- I , in theory, never should have known anything about- crossed my path in the subculture of fusion dancing, and was supposedly a "fixture" (at least in his own twisted little mind) in the BDSM world. I'd already established there was a definite crossover with said dance subculture and BSDM- including predatory assholes in my own unfortunate experience . With these thoughts in mind, I figured , why not start with integrating into both of these subcultures that I authentically enjoyed anyway?

Getting social AND furthering my secret research project on sadistic hypnotist and cults; I love multi-tasking.

Starting Fresh(-ish)

I found myself conveniently dwelling in a lovely central and well recognized Cali city that was driving distance from arguably the national mecca of BDSM and was itself rumored to be the *capital* of human trafficking in the whole damn state, so I was sitting pretty research-wise. Also, I looked it up and wouldn't you know it? They had a lovely, thriving dance scene of exactly the subculture I was seeking both for psychological catharsis and my rapidly growing little project.

So, armed with a fun new pseudo name, burner cell, shell social accounts, dyed flaming red hair and a token leather jacket- I made myself a regular. I knew there was a risk that O.G. hypnofuck (Aka: Fuckface) could have local connections (scenes are small) or that I could still be recognized, but fueled by severe PTSD, questionable alcohol consumption, even more questionable risk tolerance and utterly seething... and I do mean, seeethinggg rage, I just kind of gave zero fucks.

Because boys, let me let you in on a little secret; you can't kill someone who's already died ☺. After by the grace of God, managing to claw my way up from the depths of hell where that demon tried to drag me, I'd existed in purgatory waiting to enact some proper vengeance, some proper justice, for years -
so toying with fire? That's child's play... I've lived in it.
I've already been to the bottom, and baby, it's all up from here.

Call Me (Leather) Daddy

As for romance (and, conveniently, an intro to "the scene" locally), I didn't have to find my "him", I never really do. I've always said I could be the cops greatest fucking asset. Send me in literally anywhere, and I can guarantee the most dangerous - or at least authentically sadistic- dude in the place will approach me, no encouragement needed.

At over 6 feet tall, he was still somehow almost hard to spot right away. It was as if he was always in a shadow where no shadow seemed to exist before.

He was clearly Samoan with creamy dark skin. He had an intriguing mix of rigid (almost) scary and giant teddy bear qualities to him. He was well groomed, but still had an air of wild. This was exemplified by the tattoos sprinkled up his chiseled arms, the long black locks that framed his cut jaw and the 4 inch scar on the left side of his face that laced its way from his high cheek bone all the way down to just above his perpetual flirtatious smirk. His mouth said "come here"... his eyes said, "I dare you".

He was charming, dark, mysterious.

Also, as it would turn out (as I do love a dare), he was clearly a bit disturbed in an uncomfortably arousing way, a bit narcissistic in a (mostly) harmless way, gifted in the art of persuasion in a subtle and irritatingly skillful manner, dominating and yeah, utterly intoxicating.

Just my type, but also I thought, perhaps a bit too eager to deduce if I had any friends or connections in the city?

"No one? What about in the state?"

The touch of leather paid off apparently, not that
I'd really needed it as, like I said, I apparently
have a "gift".

Side note:

I mean no judgement. I do legitimately like leather,
and chains make me crazzzy- but have you ever thought
about how eerily appropriate it is for a sadist rich
subculture to have a fixation, a fetish even, for
wearing the dried skins of other mammals???

Just saying, kind of Buffalo Bill if you really
think about it- or, at very least, very on brand...

but I digress.

I knew he was kinky the first time we met up alone...
mostly because he told me within the first 5 minutes
of our fist drink- I mean my 1st drink with him, he
was sober for almost 2 decades. Also, he was 15 years
my senior.

The drink was his idea, I wasn't sure if it was a
convenient way to unlevel the playing field instantly
(or think that he did, as he sorely underestimated my
tolerance if so), or merely an unfortunately
incredibly accurate deduction of my very functional
alcohol-related coping mechanisms. In either case, I
certainly wasn't complaining.

I was instantly drawn to him in a terrifyingly
authentic way. Something in his soulful brown eyes
called to that deeply dysfunctional part of me that
wants to heal seemingly hurting men... who
typically, in actuality, are the ones hurting others
-

namely me, historically speaking.

The moment I felt sinkingly sure that he might be trouble?

It wasn't when he straight up told me that he was a ("nice") sadist, no, that was too easy.

It wasn't when he told me he lived a "poly, leather lifestyle", despite nearly spitting out my freshly ordered Negroni, as he loudly announced this at the bar, similar to how one might mention they liked dogs on a first date.

I wasn't really that concerned when he ordered for me on our actual first date or when I found he had a machete under his mattress (though to be fair, so did I).

Sure, I did start to feel a bit squeamish when I found out that he had a couple of Glocks in a box in the closet... which naturally, he made sure to both point out and also strongly suggest that I hold the first time he took me up to his dimly lit room.

Side note:

He lived in a (literal) haunted house, that had a very evil supervillain meets gothic castle vibe. Which- as it turns out - used to be a fucking brothel... so I suppose that makes sense. Also, his room had a four-poster bed, flanked with ropes and silk robes on each lower end.

But yes, when I was sure that he could be trouble, was probably in his dimly lit bedroom in the aforementioned (actually) haunted house. Specifically, my concern sprouted post me telling him my list of hard lines and including knife play...

and after this clearly outlined and actually quite
short list of absolute NO's, when I found him tying
me up to that four poster bed and running a Samari
sword blade across my skin while I willed myself not
to scream- as I figured he would have clearly loved
that, you know, with the sadism and all.

Well, I suppose it was then, and post aforementioned
unwelcomed "surprise" sword play, when he - after
untying me- explained the misunderstanding came
because I "didn't specify swords... just knives".

He suggested I should have told him to stop, but
thanks to trauma and an uncomfortably thorough
understanding of sadism (or at least "the type I'd
met prior to him") I had been concerned screaming
anything would have only increased the likelihood
that it continued.

So thus, I had instead resorted to staying perfectly
still while silently praying that I wasn't about to
be sliced up like fucking sashimi.

Audible scream or not, I felt pretty sure my eyes and
all other non-verbal cues were shouting "What in the
actual fuck??".

I'd later hand him a list of all sharp instruments I
could think of to add to the "NO list", adding with
a smirk "just to avoid further confusion".

Spyder was indeed a true sadist, who I made the
mistake of originally assuming was another sick bird
who I needed to "heal".

I figured it was all show, at first. But I soon
learned that there was much more to him than a sick
bird, and (perhaps?) much more to him than an
average sadist.

Sure, his years on me had afforded him an apt opportunity to practice the "art" of seduction and- admittedly- also to some extent perhaps a persuasion that bled into straight up manipulation if he didn't check himself. The latter was both somewhat off putting and annoyingly impressive (to some extent) at times.

Yet despite his nature and "skills", his tendencies, I guess the most intriguing, confounding part of Spyder was that he did actually seem to check himself... at least most of the time,

at least at first.

A self-regulating sadist?

Could it really be?

If so, I thought, he may just be my dream man.

Irritatingly enough, despite any worries, despite being smack dab in the middle of an objectively dangerous research project and low key in hiding, nothing seemed to remove my attraction to him- because life/trauma, I guess, and power dynamics?

Or maybe just those damn sexy, dark brown, anti-socially dominate eyes.

Still, he wasn't all leather and darkness, he also had a set of equally endearing very "un-sadist like qualities". For instance, he enjoyed slurping a steady consumption of diet cherry cola, typically with one of the many colorful bendy straws he kept stows of in his messy kitchen drawers. He had two dogs which he adored, but they weren't Mastiffs or Pitts like you might expect from someone so "brooding" but rather two gregarious golden doodles named "Snickerdoodle" and "Marshmallow".

The latter two may have also been sadists in their own oddly likable way, as they seemed to enjoy subjecting Spyder to public humiliation via eating shit (literally) whenever the opportunity arose in an especially populated or bougie area.

Yes, on multiple occasions, I watched these pooches enthusiastically scarf down a corgi's or angry Chiwawa's hot, gooey excrement as Spyder raced over in attempt to stop them, a string of obscenities trailing close behind him. I didn't bother hiding my squeals of laughter- despite my full knowledge I would undoubtedly sorely pay for it later.

Also? Early on I had noticed a huge stash of theater sized boxes of hot cinnamon candies by his bed side. I had at first, been staring at them, wondering what deviant act he perhaps had created with them. As I watched him gleefully rip open a box and start devouring handfuls, I discovered that he actually merely had an incredibly addictive sweet tooth.

He liked to school me on fancy hair products regularly. He owned a pair of lilac crocs, and he couldn't fall asleep without a background of nature documentaries.

I contemplated calling it off, but my attraction to him was too genuine and only bolstered by this intermingling of both dark and charmingly dorky qualities. The draw to him was too powerful to guarantee I wouldn't be suckered in. I knew getting mixed up with anyone seriously would only be a distraction to my project, but my curiosity got the better of me.

My mission was still clear, but the role of my involvement with him? How serious I'd allow it to become? That was murky at best. Still, despite the growing confusion of what the boundaries of this- whatever it was -entailed for me, I WAS learning new things almost daily as we got closer, things that filled in the gaps of many of the topics and the groups I was researching. It was undeniable he had useful information, and he wasn't shy about sharing at least some of it, as he did often talk of his long-standing ties to the social BDSM scene. The information he gave me was giving me huge gains in where to put my energies and filling in gaps that would have been challenging to fill otherwise.

I didn't really ever think he was directly involved in what I was researching, more that he was probably into some of the groups and activities on the outskirts of what I was actually seeking. Perhaps this made me start to let my guard down a bit too much, but perhaps that same lowering of the guard is what made him feel comfortable sharing what he did. Some of my questions were vaguely strategic in theory- but also organic and genuine in my very real growing attraction to him and interest in his life.

I felt that I needed to know more about the organized BDSM world, the "public scene" to understand where (if anywhere) that it intersected with predatory hypnosis groups, but to be honest, I also just found it fascinating. In a lot of ways BDSM is all about playing with idea of lines - of new space between them that was previously undiscovered, unconsidered.

Obviously, there's a huge range - some people just want to play with ropes and silk ties, others want to string people up with hooks and have slaves- and everything and anything in between. Thankfully, Spyder had seemed to run the gamut, in information at very least.

Soon, I'd even learn of auctions. These events weren't auctioning cars or collectibles though, they were auctioning off people... their subs it's said, but more accurately perhaps, their slaves. The "sales" were either for the evening, for good or sometimes for a particular sex act or service. They were auctioned off for money that supposedly went to help fund The Association. At first, Spyder didn't indicate he was part of such activities... but he would later allude to being involved in the past, similar to how a normie might recall seeing a good movie with an ex.

Sometimes Spyder would tell me things he'd done to past subs, which often resulted in a confusing mix of fear and excitement.

I mean, perhaps just fear actually - but I've always had a few wires crossed... and life has done more to further fuse this disfunction rather than untangle it. My personal theory is that it's some kind of internalized coping mechanism or evolved survival technique from being in so many temporarily unescapable situations that mixed fear and arousal, but who's to say.

As for Spyder's overshares, why was he telling me anyway? Establishing warped normalcy perhaps? A tease of his intentions for me?

Exciting the very mix of emotion I was experiencing? Was it a test to see how I'd react?

Or perhaps just an innocent display of what his "normal" was, an honest attempt to share his world.

He always got that same oddly sweet almost, pure? Look of playful happiness when he talked about toying with humiliation or pain. It didn't even look sexual- that was the most confounding, chilling and strangely fascinating part. He just looked genuinely joyous and calm when he talked about it... like a normie might look while retelling a story of a great bike ride or seeing a beautiful flower.

I felt the confusing feeling, that normies would call "fear"- apparently- but seems to be hardwired with curiosity and arousal for me... because life, and sadists, and masochism?

He would openly admit to deeply wanting to hurt me, in many different ways, but maintained that he didn't want to harm me... distinguishing "harm" from "hurt".

I -at first- considered this distinction intriguing, thought provoking even. As I'd start to reflect on it more alongside my history, however, I'd have to seriously ponder if this was just a case of pretty semantics.

Because that magical line break between what distinguished "harm" from "hurt"? In my past experiences, it seemed first to be jumping down the screen every time I turned around ... then it seemed more dotted and blurry than solid... and finally, it didn't seem to be there, at all .

Could I trust that he would continue to truly keep his darker tendencies at bay, that he'd defy my experience and be the one sadist who didn't want to "actually" hurt me - er- harm me? Could I trust myself? That I could continue to keep my own, completely opposite but horribly compatible slants under control? And not let my experiences, my "programming" from other sadists silence my "NO" when needed in the moment? Could I trust he'd respect my "NO" regardless of when it came without punishing me for it like everyone else had? Equally importantly, could I trust him to consider my experience and my trauma and watch for both verbal ad non verbal cues?

Could I trust him to not take advantage of me, and the state I'd been left in?

I didn't know, but I sure as fuck hoped so.

Semantics aside, I couldn't deny the immediately obvious- and like I said, it's not like he was either- he was literally telling me that he wanted to hurt me.

I should have been scared,

but I was just hopelessly hooked.

"I Like Dead Things"

I had seen the collection of skulls on his mantle in
that old, dark, haunted house of his. There were some
large and some small- all appeared to be animal -
much to my relief. Upon his seeing my notice, he
casually shrugged with a smirk, "I like dead
things," he offered.

There was that fun, confusing feeling in my stomach
again. He went on to explain how there were a variety
of ways to strip the bones of flesh in taxidermy. He
motioned to a book on his nearby shelf, entitled
"Agents of decay", which turned out to be a forensic
entomology guide of sorts - that detailed what
insects were most efficient at eating and decaying
the flesh off of a carcass. He said he had been
researching where he could get his hands on a few
specific species to aid in his "projects".

"I see carcasses all the time in my work: deer,
sometimes foxes or coyotes". I offered, attempting to
firmly ground our discussion of "dead things"
squarely in the animal kingdom. I went on to tell
him about a mountain lion feeding ground that I'd
stumbled into the previous week. I joked that I
should have given him a call to come collect what he
wanted of the remains of the deer.

"Yes, you should have ... we all would have come; I
would have brought a small army of us." he trailed
off with a strange, slightly ominous smile .

He had said that he and his ex use to run a dungeon
locally a few years back. He even showed me where it
had stood. Apparently, it had been shut down due to
some misunderstanding about what went on there. He'd

told me, with the same strange, far-off smile, that
their colors at the dungeon had been "Yellow, white
and dead things", how "you can't use wooden stocks -
because when people pass out from the pain of impact
play, their body goes limp... and necks snap under
the pressure". He said it all with a strange mix of
flatly factual and vague hypothetical air, which
made nailing down any finite details- or determining
if he was speaking in fact or hypothetical-
challenging to impossible. The confusing feeling
paralyzed me from pressing the issue further.

The following week, I came across another nearly
clean deer carcass along a suburban street - clearly
another victim of one of the cougars that the fires
had driven closer to humanity.

Fuck, did it ever feel like I was being hunted by
predators on all fronts.

I passed by the poor creatures remains at first,
shaking my head- until a thought struck me.

I went back to my truck to retrieve a plastic bag.
Upon returning to the carcass, I looked to either
side, and -once satisfied I was indeed alone- I
stepped on the third vertebrae of the bony neck. I
slid my hand into the bag, and snapped the neck
bones, wrenching off the head with surprising ease. I
slipped the head into the bag, and my hand out, and
double knotted it at the top.

With a slight tremble, I slung the bagged remains
into the back seat of my truck, and rolled out.

Later that night, I went over to his old, dark,
haunted house again. In one hand I held the bag with
the booze only I would be imbibing. In the other hand

I held an additional bag, which housed the heavy "gift" I had brought him.

He looked curiously at the latter as I approached. I smiled a red lipped grin - "I brought you something dead," I offered, our breathing silhouetted like dragons' smoke signals in the icy dark air. As I slung the bag towards him, his eyes widened - and for a second he looked unsure of what to say... unsure of what was in the bag. Was he worried? Or excited? Or merely calculating how to respond?

"It's a deer head" I offered, killing the moment of suspense with a smirk.

He seemed very pleased, excited even by this, as he praised my efforts and excused himself to his shed to store it "with the others" he had to work on.

"Good Chaos"

He asked me a lot of question about where I fell on
the alignment chart (apparently referencing a chart
used in D&D to describe or assign a character's
moral/ ethical qualities and views).

I'd never heard of this chart, but it made a lot of
sense to me. The quadrants, if you will, were
composed of categories describing evil, good and
neutral- and also chaotic, neutral and lawful. The
idea is, basically, that everyone is some combination
of these qualities and can be summed up (at least
somewhat) by a pair of two words from each of these
6 categories. We determined I was a chaotic good type
of character, and he was more of a chaotic neutral
perhaps, but who really knows?

What did "chaotic good" really mean? I guess (in
theory) that you have a strong ethical code that
doesn't bend, but that unlike a "lawful good",
you're open to do things other people won't to uphold
it. Where on the spectrum of "heroes" verses "anti-
heroes" did this place me? I have no idea; maybe I
was something else entirely.

I knew I had no problem or qualm doing what needed to
be done to protect myself and my friends, my
community, even if it involved wiping someone else
out (or being wiped out), but I hoped to God it never
came to that, because I sure as hell wouldn't enjoy
it.

I didn't believe I would regret it or feel remorse if
I absolutely had to do it, if it was kill or be
killed... but I sure as fuck wouldn't enjoy it.

I knew there were others who perhaps wouldn't be able to do what needed to be done or, if pressed to, would hesitate or doubt themselves.

There were still others who would only act on deadly means if "justifiable" but would undoubtedly also enjoy it to some extent- perhaps those who were self-regulating but had sadistic tendencies or the hypothetical "self-regulating sadists" I was becoming skeptically aware of.

Then there were those creatures who just enjoyed wiping people out for no reason other than their own sick entertainment and pleasure: the real monsters- those who weren't necessarily sadists but were undoubtably cruel for the sake of being cruel.

Spyder though, he seemed (in my opinion at the time) to be in the self-regulating bunch. He'd never hidden the fact that he was a sadist, which I oddly respected in some ways. Could it have been a manipulative tool to evoke a false sense of security? A "double blind" if you will?

Absolutely, but it could also just as easily have been someone who knows their tendencies doing the honest and ethical thing in "warning" the person they're about to engage with as to what they're getting into to. Or, similarly, it could have simply been him being completely honest, and "clearing his conscience" ... justifying his future acts on me in his own mind.

And I suppose regardless of intent, functionally, it could easily be all of the above.

Regardless, it was a first for me- someone just telling me that they got turned on by inflicting pain- as most sadists I knew would never admit it much less volunteer it out front.

He maintained he was a "nice sadist". I responded to this with a nervous laugh, mostly because I felt both incredibly skeptical that this concept really existed, and also because I secretly earnestly hoped that it did.

As to all the questioning, I guess it felt like he was figuring out what category that I fit into. "But why?" I pondered. Was it to know how to align himself best? Or perhaps to tell what role I would fit, a chaotic neutral partner or a chaotic good submissive... possession?

I'd originally suggested an open, casual arrangement rather than monogamy or "poly". He was poly but not interested in monogamy or "casual". Monogamy or anything "serious" was out of the question for me anyway, given my focus on the research project at hand. Though, if I'm being honest, perhaps the research project was a secondary reason why I was avoiding any relationships of a serious or emotional nature for the time being.

I'd been burned- bad- by a reckless arsonist, and I just wasn't sure I could take something going that wrong again.

The thoughts of white picket fences- of closeness- that used to fill my daydreams as a child, sent me into a full-blown panic attack in my current road ragged state.

Oddly though , the more I got to know Spyder and his upside-down world of organized chaos, the safer I felt getting close. I think it was just all so

insane, it made feeling things, closeness—even love—
feel safer, feel less impossible.

I told him one day, about the panic attacks I got
when I drove thru the minivan laced streets of
suburbia.

He laughed and replied, "I'll paint your white picket
fences black".

I think that's when I started believing that he was
my kind of chaos...

my kind of hero.

That's when I started dreaming that maybe, just
maybe, he could be my own real-life "anti-hero".

Burning (a) Man (?)

In those first few months, we gradually got closer
and closer- yet, despite my growing feelings and only
increasing attraction to Spyder, I still couldn't
seem to put myself completely at ease with him. There
was just this nagging feeling of, something... a
darkness? But I couldn't tell if it was coming from
inside of him , or merely a cloud that he was
carrying with him... something he was a victim of.

I couldn't tell if he was haunting or just haunted.

We sat atop the hotel pillow top mattress, draped in
those flawlessly oversized white comforters. We had
just gotten back from a breezy evening stroll and
dining on gnocchi and the catch of the day- the
latter he insisted on critiquing to no one in
particular in that special, peculiar way that was
somewhere between dorkyily endearing and
narcissistically mortifying.

I had just handed him a mint tea and poured myself a
stiff G&T. We cradled our Styrofoam cups and each
other as we watched a forensic show flash on the
screen before us.

I was constantly amazed at how "safe" he made me feel
being "emotional", "cuddling" even (despite my
continued inability to say any of the above without
quotation marks) . It's as if his "crazy", his
chaos made "vulnerability ", closeness, "intimacy"
feel safe... feel approachable.

As I was drifting in and out of conversation and my
own thoughts on the aforementioned new found "safety
" with unlikely accomplices , something on the screen

- or rather his sudden fixation on something on the screen- caught my attention.

It was a story about a burned body.

I looked at his eyes closer, and realized that he wasn't actually fixated on the screen at all, it was something beyond it.

After a few moments of notable silence and without provocation, he spoke ... his eyes and mind seemingly somewhere else far away.

"It's not that easy to burn a body... It takes hours ... I mean HOURS."

I felt that familiar feeling quelling up inside my core. I was "scared?" -

is that the word?-

to wake him from wherever he was drifting. I didn't ask any questions... because, honestly?

I wasn't sure I wanted to know the answers.

Still, despite this strange feeling of instinctual surety that the man I was about to fuck had likely been speaking from firsthand knowledge in his dark comments of body burning techniques, I had another strange feeling, another strange surety.

I, for some reason, felt in my core that if he had committed an atrocity like burning a human corpse - perhaps it had been for a "good" reason.

Why on earth would I assume that? What on earth would constitute a "good reason"?

I guess it was just, he didn't have any looks of pleasure or excitement when he made the comment... he looked genuinely traumatized.

I figured if it happened, it had to have been a good reason or an accident perhaps, not that either would necessarily make it "ok".

As for good reasons, I mean if someone touched his little sister or something perhaps ... that actually seemed plausible, and in the court of public opinion, also possibly understandable.

Alternatively, I told myself that maybe he was just posturing, being "dark". So, I just let it go, but I guess it never completely let go of me.

I Fell In L--- With An(other) Arsonist

Despite the disturbing hotel comment, his mention of
things like flogging as a means of breaking open
blood blisters on the backs of people - he had
(consensually) beat with harder instruments , and
repeated mention of breaking the skin and scarring as
an acceptable risk in a day to day sexual
relationship-I was drawn to him, horribly- genuinely
- addictively , drawn to him (and not just sexually)
in a way that somewhat terrified me.

I'd have to be careful, because though I was going in
with eyes open, every good fiction is based on some
truth, and the truth was he was just my type:

dominating to an utterly concerning level, scary in
that special authentically dysfunctional way that
spoke to the sick interweaving of fear with arousal
that a lifetime of abusive fucks had awarded me
with... oh, and - naturally - a sadist, which
thanks to both my streaks of masochism and my
history of utterly warped "normalcy" - felt in a
twisted way, just like home, or at very least house.

To be fair, a sadist could no more help his wiring
of arousal with inflicting pain and fear, than a
masochist (such as myself) could help the wiring of
arousal and selective forms of experiencing pain or
"fear".

The wiring is there whether we want it or not, and
rarely (if ever) completely disappears- regardless of
our efforts. I will say, however, that "nurture" or
the acting on said tendencies- whether voluntary or
not- can further hardwire said tendencies.

Where's the line, the distinguishing between the experience or "nurture" we encounter throughout life and the "nature" or innate tendencies we're born with? That's a trickier question to answer, perhaps a blurrier line to distinguish.

In the case of consensual encounters, regardless of nature or nurture, there is a necessary element of self-regulation for both parties. The obvious difference in self-regulation in a masochist verses a sadist is that the former only endangers themselves and the latter, by definition, endangers the life and well-being of another. Was this element of a mutual responsibility of self-regulation the rationale behind Spyder's rather off-putting comments regarding his overstepping my boundaries being "my fault" if I didn't stop him ?

Perhaps.

I did understand his reasoning to some level, even if I found it to be both off-putting and intrinsically flawed. It was, I argue, intrinsically flawed because, a Dom-Sub relationship/dynamic, is by its very nature un-equalizing ... a power exchange. Along with this power exchange, a Sub- a masochistic one in this case - gives the Dom - a sadistic one in this case- selective power that comes with increased responsibility... increased liability.

Once a scene, or even relationship for that matter, begins between the two parties, once the sub has clearly communicated their boundaries... it's up to the Dom to respect those boundaries, to resist the urge their innate tendencies may present to push those boundaries, to resist abusing the power they've been given.

There's that and the simpler reasoning that if your actions can potentially affect someone outside of yourself negatively, then you automatically have a higher ethical responsibility to self-regulate.

Some would perhaps call a sadist a monster by mere nature of his desire, but I disagree.

I mean, how hard must it be, what a burden it must be to have to constantly self-regulate an innate desire to hurt ?

Desire, innate tendencies, those don't make a monster ... the method of acting on those tendencies, the intent, the lack of self-regulation is what makes a monster - whether sadistic or not.

That being said, I understand that to some, the mere perpetual desire to hurt would be enough to warrant not getting mixed up with a sadist.

I get it, I mean would you let an arsonist tend your fire?

Some would say of course not, but maybe some of us counter, who else better knows how to handle the flames? Maybe you don't leave him alone with them, maybe you keep in mind his tendencies- but, he understands the fire, appreciates its beauty perhaps more than anyone else.

Maybe he's self-controlled enough to channel his nature into something positive, as long as it means he gets to gaze undisturbed into the allure of the flames.

Sure, it could end in tragedy, in chaos, in a blaze of glory... but if your fire burned hotter than most could handle? Well, maybe you're willing to roll the dice.

The only catch in this lovely, offbeat fairytale?

Fire craves

-needs-

oxygen.

It needs to breathe... it cannot ever be fully contained, much less controlled.

If you try ? Arsonist or not, you tend to get burned.

Spell Bound

He pulled out an antique fork with the inner two prongs bent into the shape of a heart in the center and the two outer ones curved into a vine like patterns bent outwards.

"Put out your arm" he more commanded then asked. I hesitatingly, extended my right arm. He gave me that charming smile that somehow always had a touch of both coy and playfully threatening, as he bent the fork around my small wrist. When he realized it was still too loose, he insisted I keep it on my arm as he clamped a massive set of plyers on the band encircling my arm and forced it as tight as he could around me.

My arm started to tremble at the very real concern that the plyers may slide to the side and clamp down on my wrist bones. Though they didn't, I was struck by how much he seemed to enjoy watching my obvious concern ... and how he -equally obviously- did not share it. Perhaps he just knew how good he was at controlling something, at controlling himself, when he wanted to.

It was a beautiful bracelet, but it also hurt if I moved the wrong way in it-

Leave it to Spyder to clamp something eccentrically beautiful onto me that both bound me and regularly caused me pain.

Yet it was so beautiful, and sweet in an odd way.

He'd openly talk of the amount of pressure you had to utilize to break human skin with your bare hands, as he stood grasping my wrists against the wall and kissed me. He'd mention with that same boyish smile, "that time" he took a guy's eye out in a gang fight he tried to break up between skin heads and Samoans.

He'd "joke" about how he thought it'd be fun to have a "roofie roulette" party (a concept created in his own creative mind , but if you guessed it involves a party centering around a CNC style gang "rape" of an unconscious "friend" , chosen via the voluntary ingesting of a cup that may or may not contain a roofie, you would be pretty on the money).

Oh, and sometimes he'd entertain aloud the risk of accidently cutting me open with phrases like "opening you up". How would he manage to accidently "open me up" ? Well because he loved knife play, of course.

I was coming to the uncomfortable conclusion that this fact terrified me—

That it terrified me, not because it was objectively dangerous (be that as it may), but rather, because it made my pupils dilate rather than constrict. I didn't want them too, but they did.

Maybe Spyder didn't really scare me,

what he unlocked in me— sometimes— did.

Well, that and his aforementioned slants towards complete "ownership".

His interest in knife play didn't scare me half as much as the ferocity that filled his eyes when he grabbed my shirt by the collar and said flatly "MINE."

It was getting real:

the feelings (despite my best attempts to
compartmentalize),

the attraction,

the addiction,
and(equally concerningly) the risk.

So, What IS Wrong With Me??

Why do I seem so organically drawn to the embodiments of my own (possible) destruction??

An unobservant eye would dismiss such a question, with a dismissive blanket answer which (perhaps) betrayed their own privileged (lack of) experiences:

" You like the drama " or "You like the bad boys" .

A more observant, experienced (or at least empathetic) viewer might recognize it as rooted in trauma rather than drama,

And although the latter would be accurate, it'd also be lacking a few additional important influences.

Namely, while trauma and the accompanying warped normalcy play a key role in this (potentially) life wrecking tendency, it's not the whole.

I've realized, the last year or so, that there are three primary additional reasons I fall for (actual) sociopaths and sadists with anti-social tendencies;

1) I appreciate their attention to detail. They notice everything, which thanks to a natural predisposition mixed with massive trauma induced hypervigilance, so do I. Unlike "normal", "healthy" humans who mostly have zero reason or want or tendency to notice every little detail of everything compulsively, sociopaths (and generally disturbed people) also see "the whole world" or at least the same world that I do and there's something "normalizing" and oddly reassuring in that semi "shared" experience.

I don't appreciate, however, that the "bad ones" fail to use their observational prowess for good or even ambivalent means and-instead- employ it for their own self-serving and manipulative purposes (frequently with a sadistic streak) merely for the brief ego boost and relief from their eternal boredom that it provides.

2) I appreciate their disgust with most of humanity, and that we can skip the toxic positivity bullshit and agree to the (sort of) obvious, that most people are self-serving shit. This makes me and my life experiences feel understood and safe to share, because frankly when speaking to someone who still says "most people are good" it's a *bit* difficult to connect, as we are apparently living on different planets.

I don't appreciate, however, that the worst ones don't respond to this reality with rebel justice or optimism and charity in the face of a rotting universe. They don't respond with a determination to fight the destroyers of the world and defy the odds if for nothing else than at least for the fucking spite of it. They instead of vowing to never become what they hate or what hurt them, instead of vowing to FIGHT till the bitter fucking end with middle finger up and head down hustling-

instead, the worst ones respond with callous, even calculatingly cruel, nihilism. They use the fact that most people are shit as "justification" to be twice as reprehensible and evil as whoever wronged them; they choose to take out more good people instead of fighting for them.

It's an utterly despicable and just plain disappointing response, frankly.

3) I appreciate that- unlike their similar but distinctly different fellow pathology-psychopathy- that sociopaths (and those with anti-social tendencies) still have emotive responses, sort of. And that they are frequently masters at making you feel like the most special person on earth -

until you cross them in any way I mean.

Because what could feel more special than having someone who despises humanity somehow fixate obsessively and affectionately on YOU?

I don't appreciate, however, that in far too many cases, these emotive reactions only seem to extend to themselves and to people they view as their "property". In the case of the latter, the emotive reactions is a mere iteration of the former; they don't mourn for you , they mourn for the damage to their own ego in response to someone playing with their "toys".

And that intoxicating attention, fixation, they offer at first? Its intensity is equally throbbing in both directions; if they obsessively "love" you, they will obsessively loath you with equal vigor and effort. What could trigger this swift swing in direction of affection?

Number one would be if you cross them in (literally) any way. Sometimes you don't actually have anything to do with it, but rest assured, you will pay for it regardless. That clerk looked at you too long? Well, you made eye contact with them as you handed them your money so it's really your fault... and the games begin. They can't control everyone, and it drives them insane, but they can control you - or so is their logic. So, you become the punching bag they use to take out their fury on the world. You pay for the "crimes" of everyone else merely by extension of being in arms reach.

If you dare to challenge them? That's the 2nd way to ensure you are hated, and probably doomed. If you challenge their decisions or behavior, you are no longer an extension of themselves, no longer that lovely possession... things aren't supposed to talk back, after all. You will be punished, and it will be "your fault".

Even if you apologize, they'll never really forgive you. They'll just play with you - scalding the ground where you crawl with a magnifying glass, just to watch you squirm until they kill you slowly with a giggle.

Lastly, occasionally, they may find reasons to hate you if you just start to bore them. Maybe you're not playing their games, ceasing to amuse them ... maybe you're too self-assured to feed their constant need for reassurance, maybe they just want to change the channel because they refuse to adjust their TV settings so no matter the show, all they see is static.

They're perpetually bored.

In closing, I'm drawn to sociopaths and the like not only because my first -everything- was one, but because (at first glance) they seem deceivingly close to empath, so close to relatable.

In reality, however, we are two types of people that had some (perhaps) mildly similar experiences but chose to respond about as opposite as possible to them.

Are we both disturbed? Undoubtedly, yes- because we've each seen and experienced some highly disturbing shit- but we all CHOOSE how and if we let that history effect our treatment of other humans.

As for the sadistic components/ individuals?

Thanks to a masochistic streak and the unfortunate natural fusing of "fear" with arousal via an actual decade of abusive sexual and relational partners (if they fire together, they wire together)-

we are a match made in fucking hell.

Also, I'm no psychologist, nor do I possess the qualifications to accurately apply proper terminology per say but I know one thing, and that's that, my whole damn life I've mostly dated two men- TWO.

They have come in many different colors, ages, sizes etc , but they are basically all one of two men.

They are both (undoubtedly) on the antisocial / psychopathic spectrum, but they possess important differences. Though I say two men, there is perhaps more of a gradient than a solid line between them. Allow me to elaborate:

Man #1 :

is highly reactive, explosive, usually has either past or (frequently) current substance abuse issues, can cry actual tears but they are demonstrative and usually only for themselves ... or on demand like some kind of party trick. He is more likely to be artistic, more likely to be (openly) sadistic and open about his kinks and interests no matter how shocking. In fact, he's more open about a lot of shocking things you would think he would keep to himself. His house and car are probably both a complete wreck, and he may or may not shower each day. He is openly vindicative, openly highly narcissistic and yet still strangely likable. The latter (I think) is largely due to mistaking his complete lack of regard for anyone or anything socially as "refreshing" or "confidence" or "free spirited" and from his overall self-destructive tendencies enticing your empathy. He seems passionate (if not insane), exciting , wild . He doesn't seem pretentious at first- but you will later learn that he is one of the most pretentious people you've ever met... whether it be about music, food etc. He is protective ... well he seemed like it at first. In reality, he's just unapologetically, insanely territorial and psychotically jealous. He is more likely to be a hedonist and also highly impulsive. Your entire family will scratch their heads at what the fuck you see in him, but he will make you fall madly (madly) in love with him. He is incredibly hard to kick because of his seeming contradictions, intricacies ... because he can be so human and oddly "sweet" in some moments.

He seems like he could be an antihero... like with the right guidance he COULD be.

But that doesn't mean he will.

#2 Man is much more scary.

He is controlled, and never (publicly) loses his cool. He is calculating. His house and car are immaculate to an OCD level and he takes personal hygiene to a whole new level. He is professionally a high achiever and your family and friends will

applaud you for snagging such a catch. He will be
popular, but not really have anyone who's actually
close to him- though he may oversell his
acquaintances to seem like besties. He will be a
bully in subtle ways. He will be obsessed with
appearances and probably brand names. It's unlikely
he'll be able to produce actual tears (at all), but
he will "sob" louder and more dramatically ... and
more often, than anyone you've ever met. His (lack
of) tears will pretty much always be for himself or
as a tool for distraction. He will probably be clean
cut, and try very hard to seem like an upstanding
"good guy". He is very moderate with his substance
use or completely sober. He doesn't like to talk
about what he's "into" , or if he does , it will be
incredibly vague (but don't worry, when you DO find
out, it will end up being something so horrifying
that his initial hesitancy to share will make perfect
sense). He is also incredibly controlling, but in
more subtle ways. He is more likely to be obsessed
with photos, "trophies" if you will. He will seem
like the "safe" choice, possibly that you choose to
distract yourself from the memories, the nostalgia of
man #1 that still haunt your dreams . He'll never be
as magnetic as type 1 but he seems like the "safe"
choice, a fact that is just so cruelly ironic. He is
better at hiding his scary until it's too late,
until you're trapped.

The latter is undoubtedly an insidious villain who
intentionally masquerades as a "hero".

Training Daze

It started small, he had little rituals he'd do...
little rules he'd make.

At first it was just a chain around my waist when
we'd go to dinner, he'd sort of grab it as we walked
together, which surprisingly didn't seem to garner
any concern from onlookers. He'd order for us. He'd
have me kiss the side of his face if I left his side,
when I left and when I returned.

I wasn't allowed to wear my clothes in his room,
unless I asked permission, and I was expected to do
the same when I needed the bathroom or a drink.

I was meant to wear one of the silk robes he had
hanging on the banister if I left the room during a
session, and I was required to address him as "sir".

It was hot.

Ok, it was hot to me, maybe it would have been
(probably?) concerning to someone closer to
"normal", (whatever that is).

I think it's partially that in my "real life" I'm
viciously independent, concerningly hard on myself,
driven to an exhausting level. In my "play time" with
Spyder, I could just let go for a second; I could
explore a dynamic I would never allow in my "real
life". Equally for him, our time provided a window
where he could indulge his need for control in a
"safe" environment. It was somewhat of an escape for
both of us.

Finally, he decided it was time to make me some
proper "training chains".

As I had a bit of a chain fetish, I wasn't exactly resistant (pun intended)to this idea.

I watched on as he bent over the links of chain , muscles flexing, forehead glistening, wrenching with all his might to crack the link. He grunted in irritation, as he disappeared to his garage for a moment. I felt the familiar mix of curiosity and a sensation not unlike fear. Soon, he'd re-emerged, a large contraption in hand. He wrenched the chain into it, and with an alarming whirring sound- the link snapped. He repeated the process with four smaller spans of chain- intermittently pausing to wrap the cold steel around my wrist and ankles, seemingly to measure what he was cutting.

When he'd finished, he slid an adjustable link into the end of each span, and slid one of them onto me . He said it was the chain the employees at the hardware store used to secure their personal possessions and tools- so he thought it was an "appropriate choice".

The "where-fear-should-be" sensation sank further, as he grabbed me hard, looked into my eyes with the black stones his had been replaced by and uttered simply; "There, now you're mine".

It wasn't a proper day collar, they were just chains he'd strongly suggest (if not vaguely insist) that I wear sometimes when I was at the house. Having a chain fetish, I wasn't hating the feel of chain on the reg, but there was something in the way he cut them, the way he talked to me about it, the seemingly complete ambiguity of when and why he had me slip them on- that I found unsettling... scary even?

But it was also incredibly hot - see above notes on warped normalcy and the fusing of fear and arousal.

It felt a bit like a psychological grooming thing-
perhaps mostly because we didn't really talk about
this practice or its significance. He started doing
other things, almost ritualistic things, but without
telling me or asking me directly. It felt like I was
being trained into something I had an instinct was
occurring but no explicit knowledge of, but at the
same time it was so deeply intriguing and frankly
oddly arousing, I wasn't sure I wanted to "spoil the
fun" with asking questions.

Then I found the books, not that he was exactly
hiding them... they were almost displayed on his
bottom shelf in the bedroom amidst other nick knacks
and collections.

At first, I'd thought it was endearing, that he had
such a massive collection of books. There was a
strange assortment of spiritualism, Catholicism,
Masons texts, a Bible and books on the occult. Mixed
in were books on taxidermy, anatomy and entomology
books on creatures that aid in decaying dead things.
The latter I originally found unsettling, but he
claimed it was just for his taxidermy habit. Like I
said, I'd already seen a pile of animal skulls of
all sizes in his study so I let it go. But then, I
looked closer at his bookshelf- and in addition to a
wide selection of kink related materials, I found
several books on "slave training". He'd always
maintained when it came up, that he had subs not
slaves. He had told me once if I looked hard enough
in his room, I'd find "what I didn't want to". I'd
found his statement odd and off-putting, but it
stuck in my head. Could this be what he was referring
to? If so, it certainly didn't take much "looking".

I put off asking about it, but I finally breached
the subject.

How do you even begin to ask someone that? "Hey, just curious, are you in the habit of keeping slaves? Oh, and sidebar, are you trying to groom me into an (actual) sex slave ??"

Fuck sometimes I wish things- anything- was normal.

He clearly felt my discomfort in asking and promptly denied any such practice or plans, which I suppose is exactly what I'd expected regardless.

Could "semantics" play a role here also? I mean, where really is the line between a "slave" and a "sub" ?

He'd told me about an old friend of his, who'd won a leather title several years before. He'd went on to mention that they'd visited a nearby convention together to educate students on "safe kink". On a whim, I'd looked up this friend, and discovered that along with winning said title, he'd also been involved in starting an organization called Masters and Slaves United or "MaSU" , to "encourage the acceptance of slave ownership within contemporary kink". He "owned" a slave himself. His website was actually sort of hard to find, which I had to imagine wasn't an accident.

I had an eerie concern scratching in the corners of my mind...how involved was Spyder in this particular branch of the scene? And what did that mean- if anything? Also, could modern day ICOM be hiding under a more "palatable" guise or floating seamlessly under the noses of mainstream society in the same manner that MaSU did?

Side note; MaSU maintained that all of their slave-master relationships were ethical and consensual, which seemed to technically be the case as far as I could tell- not that I could really be sure without meeting all of them.

So at first blush seems like an open and closed, technically kosher situation. I mean, if they're all consenting adults, then what's the problem? I suppose my first concern was just whether the above was true in all cases, or if there could be an inner circle of less palatable practices. Even if, however, they were all truly consensual slave -master relationships to begin with, how long can you live as a slave before it starts to affect your ability to distinguish what you really want, your ability to change your mind? Does the act of being in a slave role 24-7 in itself warp your ability to continue truly consenting? Does living as a slave groom you and subjugate you to such an extent that you lose the functional ability to know what you want on an ongoing basis?

I don't know, but I'd tend to think yes. Again, "CNC" people would assuredly disagree here. But I'd tend to think the dotted line would grow more and more solid as the years went on and coming back (fully) from that role would grow challenging to impossible.

At any rate, I thought that maybe as we got to know each other more, I could gain more understanding , answer my own lingering questions on where the lines in my own identity were and maybe, just maybe get closer to the branch of the underworld I sought in the process. Maybe I could find what I was looking for-

though that was a concept that evolved into something more complex and morphed into something both broader and more niche by the minute.

The line between love and fear, research and real life
- it was morphing, flexing , jumping - and starting
I feared , to fade away.

...

Two things I'm convinced of : good fiction always
has some base in reality, and reality is always odder
than the fiction it inspires.

Sometimes reality is not only outrageous, but also
dangerous... too dangerous. In a fact-based fiction
(a "faction") where does fact end and fiction begin?
Where's the line? Is there one? Is it more of a
blurred stroke of a murky brush? Is it more of an
abstract painting than a neatly typed out story?

I'm not sure,

Maybe no one is.

...

I Wanna Run Away

So yeah, ok "maybe" I moved out of the city without telling him (or anyone) where I was going.

And MAYBE yeah, ok, "maybe" I was still making midweek and weekend trips into town to see him and attend social functions and wiping my GPS history and keeping my 2nd burner hidden, all to keep up the loose façade that I sill lived in town.

Was I scanning my car for air tags before I headed home to my hideout? Ok, I mean yeah- of course.

Sure, I changed my number and gave him a burner number and wiped all my social media accounts and cut all other close local contacts.

But I wasn't freaking out... I wasn't, okay?!?

Spyder told me he loved me,

and I said it back.

I think I actually meant it.

Whether he did also- in his own strange way- is debatable perhaps to some, but I'd argue not entirely out of the realm of possibility. I suppose it would depend on one's definition of the word "love". I mean he "loved" twice baked chocolate chips cookies, the ones that he bought by the bag rather than the dozen, broke into pieces, and gleefully devoured.

Ahh, semantics.

I mean, to be fair, I guess we all utilize those to some extent, at some point in our lives.

I, for instance, had just said "I love you" to someone who invoked the compulsion to scan my car for trackers and who I felt the need to hide my city of residence from. Did that say something about HIM, what my experiences had done to ME - or both? Perhaps there's things we believe, we say in earnest, with one part of us- that some other part of us isn't quite able to fully articulate the nuance, the complexity of.

Perhaps it wasn't any doubt of the severity of his - at very least perceived- love for me that really scared me, perhaps it was the uncomfortable notion that he did actually care in his own way ... and worse, that I actually reciprocated it.

Perhaps it was the sinking sensation that I- that we- desired something that I wasn't sure existed at all, and that certainly didn't make "rational" sense between us. The sinking sensation that the four-letter word we had exchanged sounded the same but meant very different things to each of us in practice.

We were both giving our words in earnest, with sincerity I believe ... but they were just identical sponges soaked with, filled with, very different substance.

Anyway, *perhaps* all these feelings and semantics - among other factors- had something to do with my rapid retreat from the city.

What "other" factors, you ask?

Oh, no big...

Just Facing off with Fuckface unexpectedly at the
weekly dance that Spyder and I attended.

...

...

Yeah.

He breezed in the week previous, and I'd never been
more thankful to not be alone.

Thankfully, Spyder was there, and despite not knowing
why I was glaring at this "newcomer", he stepped in
front of me and shot a stare that kept Fuckface off
my tail for the rest of the evening.

Still, I saw him watching me, just like before. Every
time I looked up, he was fixated on me.

I knew he recognized me.

And despite his shaving his head and changing his
name, I immediately recognized him, those same
soulless skull cavities masquerading as eyes... the
same cruel smirk perpetually decorating his eerie
face.

It was like waking up in my own personal nightmare.

Why was he there??

Did he know about my little project?

Was he there for me??

Worse, almost, if not me- who was next?

I wasn't willing to wait around and find out.

This had gone far enough.

Maybe I couldn't take them all out , but this one...

this was personal.

As for Spyder, I suppose I just couldn't seem to square all the parts of me, with all the parts of him.

As in, I couldn't fully say with certainty exactly what kind of character I was looking at. Was he a bit macabre and unorthodox but mostly harmless, or a dangerous sadistic madman? More accurately, yet also imaginatively, stated; was Spyder an anti-hero or a supervillain? And where exactly was the distinguishing line between the two?

I started to realize that perhaps there were at least two types of anti-heroes. There were those that do the right thing for the right reason sometimes by questionable means... and then there were those who do the right thing for the wrong reason, or perhaps just their own reason entirely, by (often) questionable means. So really, I suppose, maybe there were "anti-heroes" and there were "anti-villains".

Spyder was undeniably the latter.

How far on the scale of chaotic neutral could you slide before you crossed over into straight up Machiavellian chaos??

Fuck if I know.

I do know there's some lines you don't cross, and to do so would undoubtably land you in the evil sector - be it chaotic or not. Had he crossed over any of those? I wasn't sure yet, and I wasn't sure how much longer I could justify wandering down the intriguingly spooky path to find out, but boy did I want to.

Also, to be clear;

No, obviously, I did not "trust" Spyder.

It was nothing personal; I didn't really fully trust anyone. And no, I don't think that it is sad that I "feel" that way, but I think the fact that my "feelings" have been developed via the world proving to me repeatedly that most people don't deserve to be trusted , is rather tragic.

As I've gotten older, I've realized something life changing, however.

Sure, I can't trust most people, but I don't need to. People can't be trusted , but their underlying nature- their tendencies, their character- can be, as it's frequently more consistently reliable than their word.

If you can figure out how someone ticks, as truly and as fully as possible, you can to some extent predict their behavior, no "trust" needed.

Did I "trust" Spyder?

Of course not,

but I trusted his nature.

After many hangouts, many conversations and a lot of observing, I was pretty damn sure he was what I call a "type two sadist". I feel these two groups are separated by a pretty solid white line.

There's two types of sadists , from my (unfortunate) unofficial "research" via experience.

"Type one" sadists only gain pleasure from pain if it's taken. Their approach is quick and brutal, and your best bet is to try to minimize your screams , as they will only make it last longer (see ingrained reactions for survival displayed during earlier unwanted sword play).

It can be helpful to switch reactions, as anything you seem to like or want will be decreased and anything you don't will be increased. Recovering from an encounter with one of these creatures is difficult as you have to condition yourself to survive, and unraveling that is a massive mind fuck- as your own physical reactions to stress and danger have been altered as to not fucking die.

"Type two" only gain pleasure from pain if it's freely "given" . For type two sadists, having to "take"- to physically force, to chase- it completely defeats the purpose: there's no "win", no "power" from that. Type two sees real power, real domination, in having their subject conditioned to the point of offering up their pain... of "asking for it". Type two wants to own your mind not just your body, but he'll be patient. He'll never take it. He'll play the long game; he needs you to actually want him, to want what he does. He'll never rape you, but his manipulation - his grooming- will forge so deeply into your psyche it can take _years_ to unravel you from him.

In some ways he commits the worst offense of all; he_'ll make you fall in love_.

Spyder was a type two.

So, I felt confident he would never trance me , never rape me, never force me- his nature precluded him from it. Equally, given his nature, I trusted he would protect me.

Sure, it probably wouldn't really be for me per say, but as he viewed me as his property, he would undoubtedly protect what was "his", and severely punish anyone who dared to challenge his ownership. There was an aspect of this that was disturbingly arousing ... and also an aspect that was sad and terrifying.

It was confusing.

But regardless, it was abundantly clear that I could use all the protection I could get, whatever the source , whatever the motivation.

What is our role in justice? I know self-defense isn't the same as murder ... but how far does this sentiment really go? What about the defense of others , of society ? What about proactive self-defense ? Defending yourself and your society from monsters before they have a gun to your head, before they kill or rape or "ruin" anyone else ??

In the old days they had something called "the unwritten rule". In so many words, it was a clause in the law that said if someone dishonored, assaulted , raped a woman in your family or you yourself as a woman- you had the legal right to kill them without legal consequences.

I really like this unwritten rule, but we've seen that this is one area we've slid backwards not forwards in. Just look at the type of jail sentences women who free themselves from their abusers are getting.

More maddening? Look at their sentences compared to the laundry list of femicide perpetrators, most of whom were abusers before they committed their final act of violence.

The system tells women to wait it out , wait for a
system that won't help them till it's too late...
and who will punish them if they do the job the
system is utterly failing to do.

In tribal society this shit would never stand. There
was no jury and judge- just common sense. If a man
raped a woman, touched a kid - their family backed
by the rest of the village would take him out back
and put him down like the animal he'd chosen to be.
And frankly, there's a lot of that way of handling
things that speaks to many peoples' sense of REAL
justice ... of "fuck the red tape, let's handle
business."

I can promise you one thing, if there was a bit more
tribal style justice, you can bet there'd be less of
the bullshit that escapes with technicalities or a
slap on the wrist in today's system.

At the same time, where would the line be? Wouldn't
an eye for an eye descend into chaos, anarchy? I
don't think blind vendetta or complete anarchy is the
answer... but neither is what we have.

What if an eye wasn't just for an eye? But to stop a
mad man from blinding thousands more? What if it was
an eye for a thousand? A hundred? A dozen?

Where's the line?

I don't know what the answer is, but despite its
pitfalls, I still think there's a need for at least a
touch of more creative justice than currently
exists... or at very least social accountability.
There's at least a need for a bit more actual
involvement, SELF-policing, by we the people as far

as what social norms and practices, what behaviors and crimes that we accept...that we "allow".

I do firmly believe that we should stop fucking "minding our own business" and make injustice to anyone, to any of our fellow humans OUR BUSINESS and OUR PROBLEM.

Perhaps we stop waiting for an understaffed system that's intrinsically flawed because it's made up of people-just like us- to take action , and instead; step the fuck up , speak the fuck up, and say NO MORE to the predators of the world, whoever they are and whatever they look like.

We have got to make sure justice , real justice, is carried out- one way or another.

Still, I just couldn't do it. I knew he was a threat to my life , but I suppose it wasn't imminent enough for me to "justify" it.

I've always said I prefer exposure as a means to justice over violence - but this guy was so careful. We both knew I had no "proof", no way to directly and irreprovably tie him legally or criminally to the crime. And he came to me... to MY city.

I knew what needed to happen, but found myself paralyzed.

So, I told Spyder-

not about my research project or the cults or the bigger plan to take down an underground ring of amateur hypnofucks , but I told him about what Fuckface had done.

I suppose I knew (at some level) what would happen next.

And that surety, it made me fall even deeper for Spyder.

I had realized that night, the night that my nightmare showed up, something extraordinary:

there was no one else I wanted to be by my side in that moment. There was no one else who could have made me feel so surreally calm and confident, so sure that I was safe.

I did love Spyder, and he gave me something no other man ever had:

a sense of safety.

With this in mind, after we exchanged 4 letter words, I told him I was ready for him to officially collar me too, but I made sure to remind him I was agreeing to be a sub... and that I was a Bratt not a slave.

"Don't worry, I take very good care of my things" he responded.

"I'm not a thing, I'm a person, this is an important distinction." I shot back.

"Sorry honey, we won't use that word then." He offered, with a smile.

Why People Buy Diamond Chokers For Their Chihuahuas

There was something about his calloused hands, his nails bitten past the reem of his fingertips, holding the silver... undoing the clasp...

his smirky little smile I'd grown to adore ...

feeling his rough fingers graze the nape of my neck as he slid the cool silver chain around it and smiled down at the heavy heart that hung before him.

I didn't give a shit about designers, he knew that.

He wanted the silver glove treatment, and I suppose he wanted something pretty there to validate that, yes , he did belong in this type of world.

The sales associate- like so many other women who'd jealously eye the nearly 1,000 dollar chain around my neck- mistakenly assumed his purchase was a reflection of his care for me, and admonished me while he was in the bathroom on what a "sweet" man I had to "love" me so much as to buy me something like this.

I just smiled pleasantly and vacantly agreed , as there was no point and no time to attempt to enlighten her.

Why do people buy diamond collars for their Chiwawa's?

Why do they haul them around in designer bags??

Is it because they "love" their dog so much?

Or is it because they want a pretty accessory for their pretty accessory?

Because, in actuality, they only see their dog as an extension of themselves, or worse, an extension of their wardrobe... just another thing to drape themselves in to look fashionable, to tell the world "I've made it", and here is my trophy to prove it.

The designer collar was just that, a collar.

We both knew the designer aspect was for him even though it was "for me"; I never would have let him spend that much on me otherwise.

Still, the contrast, his hard-working hands on something so smooth... that he handled so reverently, how happy it made him... something about that- THAT- made me fall even deeper.

I felt empathy, I guess. He cared so much about being treated like he was important, like he was known or rich or influential. I couldn't help but wonder about all the little things in his time on earth that could have sparked that void in him, and it was sad. It made me want to envelope him, to make him feel secure, wanted ... enough.

It made me want to pour all the things I'd never gotten into him at the sight of his preoccupation with things I've never given a damn about.

Along Came A Spyder

It's weird, Fuckface , the trancy trickster himself?
You know, no one's really heard from him in quite
some time I hear.

Shortly after the afternoon in that jewelry store
with Spyder, Fuckface just stopped going to dance
completely. In fact, it seems he hasn't been sighted
anywhere, at all.

Well so I hear, that, and rumor going around is a
"nice" sadist, may have been informed of what this
brute did to me, his lovely pet.

A "nice sadist" who REALLY doesn't like people
treating his things poorly, and also REALLY loves an
excuse to break out his knives and play some games.

For a time, we were so happy , Spyder and I .

The (presumable) action on his part to "take care of"
what was bothering me, only served to endear him to
me more. I wanted to thank him for his kindness. I
felt both that I owed him my allegiance, and also
that I wanted to freely give it.

Maybe we'd make a good duo, a solid team. Maybe if I
just leaned in, relinquished control over myself,
he'd treat me well. Maybe I'd be protected;

I'd be safe.

Fuckface was far from the only monster I had to
worry about.

With Spyder by my side, I knew I'd be safe from
anyone,

well,

from anyone but Spyder.

Boxxed In

A month or so later, Spyder took out a measuring tape with a casual comment on wanting to buy me some clothes. I told him my sizes, which he notated on a small pad, but still insisted on measuring me anyway "just in case".

We were in his bedroom, and it was a lazy Sunday morning. There was something in the way he uncurled the tape, his expression of satisfaction, the levity of his movements, the levity of his silence, the dramatic manner in which he scribbled every single measurement on the small piece of paper; it all started to make me strangely squeamish.

I suppose it felt odder still when he didn't stop with traditional measurements, and proceeded to measure EVERY part of my body.

By the time he ripped off the notebook sheet , rolled it into a scroll and placed it into a strange little cedar box, I had started feeling that (becoming) familiar, but still surprising, nausea welling up in the pit of my stomach.

I know I looked frightened , because his smile got that peaceful somewhat terrifying, yet oddly arousing set that it did when his appetite for exciting fear and the orgasmic sensation it momentarily brought was being fed.

It was far from the only behavior that would excite my concern, my confusion or his appetite, however.

Upside Down World

Despite what people perhaps assumed from the outside, the sex and kink aspect was actually not the essence of what drew me to Spyder. Sure, the freedom to explore things with someone who, at very least, I felt confident wouldn't force himself on me was great. What really drew me to him though -other than the sense of safety he provided me with- was actually his company.

Though I'm sure his carpenter hands, charming type A personality and admitted significant seniority probably reminded me at some level of my former traveling salesman father (my therapist said this is "normal"). Equally, some of his more concerning qualities (like the sadism) definitely reminded me of my first love.

However, none of these factors compared to the effect of Spyder simply being harder to freak out than any dude I'd ever known. I guess what I mean is, he listened. He wasn't scared away by the shit I'd been through. I can't 100% guarantee the nature of his motivation behind listening, but the listening- the making me feel heard in that way- it was something I really, really needed at the time. Regardless of what his motivation may have been, it was undeniable he was very intuitive. He made me feel seen.

Everything in his world was so insane, it made me feel "normal" or at least not alone.

It had been a strange "new normal" , yet it had still provided more structure - more safety - than anything or anyone else had in my chaotic last decade of survival-based decision making.

I mentioned Spyder's way with words before, "painting my white fences black" with his undeniable charm. Yet, there were the less "endearing" sound bites, that certainly seemed to dramatically increase as he grew more comfortable in his "possession" of me.

Some were simply rooted in wildly blind but probably harmless narcissism, like when he literally remarked to himself aloud; "Wow, I'm the best thing that's ever happened to you".

Was it off-putting ? Obviously - but I just rolled my eyes and hoped he was (at least partially) joking.

But towards the (spoiler) end , his less pleasant remarks took on a heartbreakingly callous flavor- with curt comebacks like; "I can't deal with this right now", in response to his previously requested communication on things like boundary violations or hurt feelings. I couldn't help but also notice that these comments seemed especially more likely to occur if he'd already gotten laid.

Also, the latter- getting laid- seemed to suddenly be the only manner he "reconnected", which felt a lot more like punishment or hate sex than anything remotely near "connection".

Even his formerly cheesy but sweet lines started to show signs that we were on very different pages, if not very different novels, entirely. One particularly sad example of this occurred on an (almost) romantic evening out on the 4th of July.

With fireworks spraying the night sky in glorious shades of red and purple, and crowds cheering all around us -I looked over at him, feeling for a moment that everything froze... feeling for a moment that I wasn't crazy for feeling what I did. He kissed me like he meant it, and then we just stood there, our breaths sending silent whispers through tiny clouds in the air between us.

Until he broke the sacred silence with: "I'm happy to be seen here with you-" uttered flatly but with a smile and a glance around us.

Ouch.

I think he actually intended it to be, expected it to be, "heartwarming". It was a shot to the gut instead, at least partially due to my knowing how genuine, how accurate, that statement truly was.

It was no secret that I often felt like a fancy handbag to him... I'd literally told him as much (repeatedly).

I suppose in some ways he saw it as a compliment to me. I think he would have taken those kinds of statements, that kind of attitude as a compliment. Maybe he saw it as such, and just couldn't get how gutting it was to someone who desperately wanted to be seen as more ... who put no value in being esteemed for social status or popularity booster merit.

I loved him. I didn't give a shit about anyone else when we were together, in those moments everyone else faded and dimmed around us.

I wish I could say that effect was mutually experienced- mutually felt- mutually possible, but it (undoubtedly) was not.

"I'm happy to be here with you-" I offered back, not attempting to hide my hurt as I said it.

I knew I was right in my sinking realizations on the nature of his affections for me; I'd just really, really, hoped that I wasn't.

I just really wished that I wasn't.

...

I always used to say we had different vocabularies, differing language construct, and I genuinely believed that if "we" could "translate" our "languages" of communication effectively, that we'd find we were, in fact, on the same page after all.

But as I got to know him better, with time, I was faced with an unsettling question:

what if it's not about language translation?

What if he was just bumbling around with vague or off sounding vocabulary as a manipulative tool in order to deduce my feelings and-when it suited him-mirror them, then attempt to slowly change them?

After all, language and redefining it is undeniably one of the oldest strategies in the book for changing someone's world view, their beliefs.

So much so, that both in major corporation's as well as cults there is a concerted effort to achieve an altered and homogenized "language", a jargon of sorts, that is drilled into the participants in order for them to "buy into" the corporation's (or cult's) way of view.

It's a framing technique.

Marketing in many ways is built on the same basic principles.

At the same time, I believe that he- at least to some extent- genuinely believed his own bullshit, but that doesn't change that it was bullshit.

Frankly, you could say the same for many cult leaders .

Still, the conviction in which this allowed him to deliver his words in- however mellow dramatic or narcissistic his diction sometimes strayed- added a lot of confusion and self-doubt and "benefits of the doubt" in me.

This was especially felt as someone who struggled with no normal to serve as a standard and little to no support system to bounce crazy off of... not to mention the complicating factor of our preestablished power dynamic.

Distinguishing Intuitive From Empathetic

Then there was the way he talked about it- what we
did...what he did... what I let him do.

A bit of narcissism is not unheard of, and
admittedly perhaps a touch of ego can feel sexy in
certain moments. His outlook seemed to reach a bit
beyond moments or scenes though.

In what manner you ask?

Some were off putting but clearly meant (somewhat) in
jest, like when he referred to himself as a "sex god".

Some were equally off-putting , but almost sweet-
like the oddly ceremonious and overly dramatic
language he insisted on using when starting a sexual
interaction.

Others were less ambivalent and more flat out
concerning.

There are two that are seared into my mind. The
first, a one off, occurred when I was inquiring what
knife play with wax did for him. He went into what
was (but probably shouldn't have been at that point)
surprising detail with seeming earnest about this.

It wasn't just what he said, it was his eyes- how
they were momentarily transfixed ... how he seemed to
almost be holding his breath with anticipation as
he said it.

The positive was that my suspicion was correct, I
didn't have to worry about him cutting me , because
accidently cutting or cutting without consent he
would see as failure. The bad thing ? Just his clear
and completely unapologetic god complex... that's
all.

No, he wasn't into knives for blood or for cutting.

He was into knives and raking them against naked skin, shaving layer after layer of melted wax off of the possessed before him, as they tried not to shake with baited breath.

He was into THAT, because he saw it as a "god-like" power.

He liked the power -the fear-that it produced, the power to instill in someone the willingness to allow him to put them in that baited breath position.

He liked knowing that he held the "power" to cut them but that he had the "power" , the skill, to avoid it by mere millimeters.

He loved how terrified it made the person underneath him , and (even more) that they laid there and "took it" anyway- "for him".

The second, equally disturbing but (much more) frequent discourse, was about pain.

I mean, yeah, he was a sadist- I knew that, and I'd seen it before.

What I hadn't seen before was the specific way he seemed to view inflicting pain.

Like, it wasn't enough to inflict it- it had to be in some way "given" to him.

Again, this was somewhat comforting in a way, I suppose, as it bolstered my theory that he was the type of sadist who wouldn't outright brute force anything, but there was also something deeply unsettling about it all.

Was there manipulation? Sure, admittedly to some level, throughout.

Was I operating on a massively trauma laden groundwork that he was dually informed of previously? Absolutely.

That being said, the "pain" was consensual, and I've never denied having a masochistic streak.

The inflicting of pain wasn't actually what was unsettling to me.

His pulling me close to him , like I was a fire to warm by as he whispered into my ear, "That's it, give it to me; give me your pain... offer your pain up to me..." and similar iterations of the same type of verbiage-

THAT'S what I found chilling, haunting.

It sounds hyperbolic, but it literally felt like he was getting energy from my pain, from being as close as possible to it, from the fact that it was "given".

There is a similarity in at least one aspect of sadists and empaths: the heightened sense of and ability to feel another's pain.

Perhaps the largest difference between sadists and empaths is what feelings sensing that pain invokes, and what they do with it.

Controlled Burn

It was impossible to ignore the slant towards slave his concept of "sub" had. It was impossible to ignore how irrevocably woven together his concept of "love" was with control... worse, with complete possession.

It was becoming increasingly obvious that I could be completely safe guarded if I would just let go ... if I'd just let Spyder possess me fully.

Still, despite how much danger I was in, the fight in me just wasn't sure I could bear bartering my human autonomy for protection or for "love",

and wasn't sure I should have to.

I'd seen it before. The men who only "love" someone they see as childlike, corruptible, unintimidating, non-threatening to their fragile ego and who doesn't threaten their lust for, their demand for, utter and complete control.

They only "love" you, when they *own* you.

But possession isn't love.

I mean sure, do you "love" your car, do you "love" your designer bag? In a sense I suppose. But you'd never take a bullet for either. You don't "respect" either; you can't, because they are objects. Sure, maybe you'd fuck someone up if they stole or damaged either, but only because they messed with your possessions-

because they damaged something that you like to use ...

because they disrespected something that you invested
in.

It would be a crime against you, not your car or
your purse.

He protected me the way that people put alarms on
their cars,

the way stores use detectors to keep out shop
lifters-

the way you keep someone from stealing your
merchandise.

I don't know, maybe it was a knockoff of "real"
love, but it was the closest thing I'd had.

And protection- regardless of its motivation- is
still protection, and God knows I needed it more than
ever.

In many ways, the smartest thing I could have done
was to stay.

Perhaps if I didn't actually feel four letter words
for him in deeper ways than I wanted and deeper ways
than he seemed to be able to understand much less
reciprocate, perhaps then I could have continued to
bask in that protection.

But that just wasn't reality;

that just wasn't me.

Scene 2

I tried to put these complicated ponderings on Spyder out of my mind, as it was time for phase two of my little project.

Having moved to the epicenter of all that is kink in the country, I was in prime position to take the information I'd gleamed and do some more unpersonal, in-person research thanks to yet another reinvented persona.

Bay area kinksters, meet "Ember".

I pulled a wisp of bright orange hair behind my ear and straightened my wig for the umpteenth time. I slipped on a sheer long sleeve top , and zipped up my combat boots over the tattered fish net before layering on another coat of dark eyeliner and black lip stick. Finally, I clipped the chain harness around my neck, and took one last look in my hair spray soiled mirror. "Here goes nothing I guess," I whispered to the stranger who stared back at me.

I told NO ONE, not Spyder, not family , not friends-

no one.

I had bought a wig online, crafted the mentioned "scene name" and did my homework.

It was an odd thrill in a way, to have a secret, even if just a secret for necessity's sake.

I'd already been to the intro sesh at the Basement, my "soft entrance to the scene "- and also where I'd first met him, the owner of the space, Osborn Black.

The aforementioned intro sesh is where I'd watched
him very obviously sniff out the submissives with
masochistic streaks- the ones who were truly new in
the sense of still harboring guilt, shame and
confusion for what excited them, the malleable and
easily exploitable of the bunch.

He paid special attention to a younger, timid,
clearly submissive girl who'd expressed being new in
town and who's only question during the event was if
Osbourn had any advice on how to get over the shame
she held for her slant. Side note, Osbourn tried not
to visibly drool upon hearing this and made sure to
exchange information with her after the event.
Preying on the vulnerable in a marginalized community
which presents complications in reporting, wow ,
what a novel thought.

After a welcome monologue that was mostly a fluff of
"insider" information that could easily be found
online with really quite minimal digging and the
vaguest interest in the subject of BDSM- he began
inquiring interests by a show of hands on a series
of kinks. He ended the list with an obvious plug for
-perhaps his real- motivation in hosting said intro
sesh. He excitedly asked if anyone had an interest in
"spiritual BDSM".

"Spiritual BDSM" perhaps the most ridiculous
combination of words ever penned and also a
conveniently ambiguous term to disguise a much more
sinister agenda. Certainly, at best, it was a
complete misnomer for what he was a part of.

But I'm getting ahead of myself. Because, though I
instinctively distrusted him from the start (a
clear attempt to control the scene, an obvious

sadist and a part of the leather world I'd had a recent unpleasant run in with)- I didn't yet know his full involvement in the bigger, darker picture. His comments about "Spiritual BDSM" at this intro sesh was actually part of what led me down the twisted rabbit hole full of things I never wanted to know but can never unsee.

This - my first "play party "- was to be more of my official debut though, the first of many nights I'd attempt to integrate myself into a public scene I'd practiced privately for decades.

Perhaps my authentic "tendencies" could actually be a help for once, instead of a mere gateway to masochistic chaos.

I'd definitely pass the sniff test in this world without much effort. There was a part of me that was doing this for more than just research I had to admit, I'd always been curious. I'd felt beckoned to the shadows of the public scene more than a few times, but I'd always resisted until now.

Was it justification? Well yes, obviously, but also useful in my research.

Was I searching for answers to the twisted puzzle I'd found myself in the midst of, or the fragmented pieces of my own identity?

Maybe both, I don't know-

but I DID know, I needed to become a regular fixture in this so called "underworld" if I was going to learn anything about the dark forces behind my own near-death experience and the players behind whatever sick game I'd nearly fallen victim too.

I parked far enough away to not be spotted by any other attendees and tightening the beige trench coat around my waist. I made my way up the street spotted with dives and abandoned buildings and turned down the alley as instructed in the invite. Finally, I approached the fenced in entrance guarded by a man dressed in all black holding a clip board.

I had used a fake name, a prepaid card and a shell email account to purchase my ticket- and of course gave an unrelated "scene" name I'd already began circulating at the kink nights I'd attended at the local goth club nearby.

My would be nearly flawless plan-could very easily fall apart in a mere instant -however- thanks to the pandemic and the newly accepted practice of checking IDs and vax cards to ensure they matched.

Yes- I know, I know- if I was a real pro, I would have just precured a phony of each - but I'm still (semi) new to my life of next level delinquency, so I couldn't risk getting called out on a sub-par fake. I mean using a scene name was the norm, and from what I'd heard this was one area where vetting wasn't really stringently enforced for most events.

My only worries were that I'd used a fake "actual" name as well as scene name to register, and I wasn't sure if that would be an issue. I just didn't know what to expect or what exactly I was walking into. I didn't know how many , if any, connections Fuckface - or Spyder for that matter- had in the scene locally, and I wasn't trying to risk more than I had to.

So, sans fake ID and using a "real" name that did NOT match my ID or vax card, I would just have to hope that superficial charm and the ludicrously small amount of clothing I had on would secure my entry without further questions. With these thoughts in mind, I casually undid the tie on my waistband and let my coat whisp behind me in the breeze as I approached. I told him my scene name and flashed an "embarrassed" smile as I quickly showed him my vax and ID. The man paused, searching the list for the name on my ID. I explained in hushed tones that it was my "first time" , so I hadn't really been sure "how all this works", that I'd used an alias because I was a bit nervous. At the notice of his slight look behind him, I threw in a little "shy" tug at my leather choker -that looked just enough like a collar to entice the interest this situation called for, but not enough to signal that I was taken - add in a downcast glance and bingo; it was a go.

He stepped to the side with a "Welcome, have a good time tonight".

Fuck, I always forget I have backup tools like small clothing and gender cliches to fall back on when my smarts and other resources are futile.

Sure, he'd know my real name now- but it's highly unlikely he was very connected or senior in this world - or that he was "skilled" in the sadistic mindfuckery I was here to silently begin to dismantle.

I'd already read that the only staff were to be volunteers, and that they got a free entry for their trouble- though, no doubt, ingratiating themselves to the senior members of the community and the illusion of power and aforementioned seniority was more likely the actual motivation for our man in black and his pals.

Everyone here wants to be "someone in the scene" or know someone who is.

Frankly, I don't get it, but I never really got it in high school either.

I guess some things just don't change.

Then again, people who "got" high school, were also probably attending weddings, baby showers or promotion parties ... and I was a divorcee who lived with her cat and hunted hypnotists for kicks. Oh, and I was spending my Friday night waiting in a dark alley draped with an orange wig and leather- so there was that.

The dark interior was smaller than I'd expected, but completely drenched in leather and metal (of both the iron as well as the musical variety). There were several rooms themed for different types of play activities. The first couple were pretty tame (the electrical play demo being the "edgiest") and mostly consisted of a fun little scaffolding bit, some mats for take down scenes and huge bean bags for aftercare and "cuddling".

The latter made me far more uncomfortable than anything else I'd see that night. As for aftercare, when engaging with strangers I mostly preferred a drink -or would have if this weren't a dry event.

I mean I get it, but I'd bet most things that I wasn't the only freak that had lightly pre-gamed before attending this little den of fun. I didn't booze enough to be affected, mind you, but just enough to take the edge off ...before - you know- potentially letting strangers flog me mostly naked while other strangers watched?

But I digress.

The next few rooms got progressively more
interesting; a human sized cage (regrettably without
the door because fire codes), a loft with a sex swing
and a queen-sized bed, and lastly -both the largest
as well as my personal favorite- an entire area
reserved exclusively for impact play and suspension.
There were St. Andrew's crosses, benches, reclining
chairs with restraints, suspension anchors and a
voyeur area to the side for an audience. The loft
room overlooked the impact area, and beyond said
impact area, there were two last rooms. One was a
room that I stayed away from, a "water sports" and
needle play area, and the other room (that I only
peaked into this time) was a darkly lit upstairs
"intimate activity " area .

I mean "intimate" may be a stretch? As there were
multiple bean bag chairs, couches, swings and beds-
but who am I to say?

What I could say- undoubtedly - was that there was
literally nothing on earth that would convince me to
sit on any furniture in that room that was not
draped in a sheet that I brought from my own sterile
environment.

Speaking of sterile, I was relieved to see that
protection was not only strongly encouraged, but
strongly enforced. Everyone brought their own toys
and wet wipes and condoms abounded - so thankfully
the risk of encountering any unwanted substances was
minimized. Additionally, and perhaps surprisingly
for some, there was actually very little penetrative
sex happening of any kind in any room- even between
couples who'd come together. There were, of course,
house safe words that would automatically stop a
scene via inviting outside enforcement, and also
plenty of dungeon monitors making sure no funny

business (that wasn't consensual) occurred. Oddly enough, in some ways, it actually felt safer than many vanilla, "normal" parties I'd been too... or even dates I'd been on, as sad as that may sound.

As much as I was enjoying myself, I had to stay focused; this was supposed to be (at least partially) business.

Primarily, I was there to learn the lay of the landscape, and perhaps start to get an idea of what I was dealing with. Secondly, well, I'd been toying with a very dangerous, kind of insane idea: using myself as bait.

As I wasn't yet sure if Fuckface had told anyone local about me (before his highly "unfortunate" disappearance, I mean), I knew it was already a possibility that some of his fellow hypnofucks may have gotten a heads up I'd be around, and in that case, they may already be on the lookout. So, I thought, why not play into it?

I thought, if I could wear my recording device and just go in seemingly "oblivious" to what they were doing, maybe they'd try to trance me while I was "wired" ... at least then I'd have pretty irrefutable proof.

The catch? I wasn't going to violate any innocent party's privacy by wearing any type of recording device in a "public" play space, party or fet night. It just seemed kinda fucked and on top of that, if the bug was found in a space, it'd not only blow my cover but land me on a blacklist and end my chances of both investigating and experimenting.

And so, I kept an eye out for a potential NLP / trancey fellow. It wasn't actually that hard. Then again, I shouldn't be surprised- predatory psychology is disappointingly predictable given the reliable narcissism and the both inability to pass up a chance to gloat coupled with the oh so convenient tendency to CONSTANTLY underestimate their opponent. Well that and the unwavering commitment to their own satisfaction and "winning" or "dominating" others at all costs, without a fleeting thought for "troublesome" concepts like empathy or conscience or morality (or in many cases even consequences) that make actual humans -by contrast - such nuanced, complicated , beautiful and unpredictable beings.

It took me all of an hour to attract one of them.

I had picked this event in particular because, though it was geared towards newbies, veterans and regulars were also welcome to attend.

With all the fresh meat, it'd be open season for anyone looking to hunt. I just lugged around my small bag with my flogger tucked inside but draping out the corner and donned my best shot at "wide eyed and innocent ". I wandered into the "social circle" -a circle of fold out chairs situated between the voyeur area and the impact and suspension play zone and sat down across from my target.

I'd already spotted him, alone and clearly on the hunt. Not horrible looking, but with an edge of incel that was impossible to ignore. He was obviously a Dom and given the gleam in his eye may or may not be a sadist - though, to be real, given the overlap (in the social scene at least) it was highly likely. He was tall, bald with a goatee, clad in black jeans and a black, long sleeve button up.

He was in his late 30's I guessed, and toted around a large, black case- no doubt filled with his tools of

choice- so it felt safe to assume he'd been around
this world for a minute.

He watched me - the same way that Fuckface had-
though in a much more obvious, seemingly less
"skilled" manner. Once he struck up a chat with me,
true to NLP creeper form, he paid special attention
to where my eyes darted as I answered his questions.
Partially as a precaution, as this was merely a
preliminary fishing and I wasn't sure of my level of
danger yet, and partially for my own entertainment, I
made sure to intentionally let my eyes vary the
direction they slid with little to no pattern. I
must admit that I deeply enjoyed his thinly veiled
irritation and confoundment at this. He'd likely
chalk up his inability to establish a clear read on
my patterns or "mental map" to my being untruthful
to his questions in some way - but that was ok, a
lot of people lie about their life at these things.

Plus, he'd probably see my self-protection as a
"challenge" and predictably be unable to resist the
temptation to "break " me .

Barf, detestable and unoriginal; could these guys be
any worse??

Me and the mystery Dom did a couple scenes and thanks
to a little charm, some on point reactions to impact
play and the burner number I gave him, he'd invite me
to several events and invertedly slip several useful
little tidbits.

The Take Over

Over the next couple of months- and while I was
playing dress up with sociopaths in attempt to get
those aforementioned tidbits- Osbourn took over. I
figured it was coming - but found myself still bit
shell shocked at the pace in which he did it.

The new kinksters seemed to know his name well, but
nothing of Society of Jane or other historically
significant organizations. Society of Jane was one
of the first kinky groups established in the U.S.
and was originally functionally a support group for
masochists. Regrettably, several years after their
establishment, they voted to allow sadists to join
also- but who hasn't fallen for the "I'm a nice
sadist though " line once ?

Oh, just me?

...

But I digress,

It was difficult not to notice the clear trajectory
the events offered in the area were taking - or that
the vast majority were hosted at his basement space
by his kinky cocktails and eatery.

What kind of events? You know, things like
"Gnosticism and coffee", "sex magick", "embracing the
shadow self", "spiritual BDSM discussion", "mental
training techniques for the slave master", "broken
and owned; how to own your sub forever", "advanced
hypnokink and brews", and that's just a small
sample.

The "spiritual BDSM " workshop had a particularly
interesting descriptor, in that it urged any members
or prospective members of O.D.O. or D.D (but the two
D's were each followed by a triangle of dots) as
well as anyone interested in Dhelema views or sex
magick to attend.

I'd already researched "spiritual BDSM" after the
intro session I attended - and found it to be a
synonym for the practice of sex magick to some
extent.

I'd researched sex magick and found it to be using
themes of ritual- often with occult themes to
"channel" the "energy" from orgasm (among other
things) to power a desired outcome or goal. Upon
further research, I found that in some circles, it
also had cross over with hypnokink and sometimes
utilized trance as a tool. Perhaps more
disturbingly, I found that at least some sectors of
sex magick also involved sadism and the infliction
of various forms of torture -to draw "power" not
only from orgasm (or near orgasm) but also from the
pain of the submissive (slave) involved.

This seemed obviously, blatantly fucked up, but given
what I'd seen of humanity, not exactly a complete
shock I guess.

Then I looked up the other term, I found they all had
ties to a fellow named Al. Drowley. And that O.D.O.
and D D were both occultist secret societies of sorts
based on Drowley's's teachings (rooted in a
spiritual belief called Dhelma). All made mention of
"sex magick" throughout and borrowed from catholic,
Hindu, kabbalah (Jewish mysticism), occultist and
Masonic symbolism and themes.

That name, Drowley, I HAD heard that name before. I hadn't looked it up at the time , or thought much of it, but a man who called himself Daruka had asked me if I'd read Drowley's teachings - and suggested I look it up.

I'd found Daruka's discourse nauseatingly predatory and sexist, and later found him to be an associate and fellow film nerd of the shitstain who'd tranced and raped me and sent me down this hellhole of an underworld to begin with - so it made a disgusting amount of sense.

Of course, I'm sure both of them whole heartedly concur with Drowley's one law, which (paraphrasing) is: "Do whatever you please".

Which has to be the stupidest mantra I've ever heard. A fanciful version of "Do whatever you please" ... seriously??

Justifying an already incredibly selfish species darker tendencies and accelerating entropy . "Do whatever you please" without regard for conscious, ethics, community and the like- removes the higher abilities that separate us from more brutish life forms and lowers humans to the state of a fucking animal.

"Do whatever you please", I argue,

is the definition of "chaotic evil" .

"Do whatever you please" doesn't believe that double yellow lines exist, but next time you're on the highway, try crossing one- I'd offer- and see what fucking happens.

I began to wonder, was this for real though, like was anyone really still a part of this O.D.O.? How exclusive was this little cult? And how serious? How dangerous? And could it be tied to a modern-day version of ICOM... or even ICOM itself?

As for the "hypno and brews" event mentioned above, I decided to pay it a little visit - well , sort of.

It was touted in the descriptor to be tailored to "intermediate and advanced practitioners", and it was "strongly suggested" you come with a bit of a showcase - something to share with the group if you will , presumably , as a subtle vetting procedure.

As I felt neither capable nor comfortable attempting any trancing and was -in theory - attempting to keep a low profile , I planned to do a bit more of a drive by.

Basically, as it promised to be all "upper level" hypno fans, I wanted to get an idea of who was involved and do a bit of digging on the guest list as it was rich with potential to overlap with my targets.

I was aware, of course, that some participants (perhaps even the majority) would be in the (mostly) non - predatory group , but there was definite overlap.

Why do I say "mostly" non-predatory? Because in the best-case scenario when we're talking mixing hypnosis with sex and kink , we're talking initially voluntary participants interested in exploring the power dynamic angle of hypno play and potentially the ability to influence levels of orgasm with hypnosis tactics.

Though these folks are not my targets or my issue, I do have ethical qualms with it as any activity which takes away someone's ability to give ongoing consent throughout the experience/ scene or sexual encounter is inherently, not truly consensual (in the purest sense).

Obviously, CNC folks would beg to differ, and we'll just agree to disagree, I guess.

My point is, though I disagree with mixing sex and hypnosis (at all) due to the fact that once someone is in trance, they are unable to truly consent or stop what is happening - My feud is not with hypnokink couples or partners , my fight is against the covert hypnosis and NLP practitioners using these tactics on unsuspecting victims.

That's why I was there; that's who I was hunting. Anyone else I found along the way , I was not interested in making beef with or trouble for.

Getting inside the event was out, and as they were only selling tickets in cash at the door the day of , so was any hope of hacking the guest list. Thankfully, it was conveniently held in a basement space of the kinky eatery I mentioned, I decided to just put on my "disguise", take a stroll and pop in for a drink a few minutes before the event was scheduled to get out. I'd sit at the picnic tables outside and have a clear view of the door by the alley that led down to the basement where the class was held .

In addition to the wig, I'd be wearing my fun new fake glasses. These added a sexy intellectual look , shielded my identity a bit more and had a tiny video camera in the lenses. It really is amazing what you can legally purchase online if you look for it.

The day finally arrived. Though incredibly nervous, I showed up and I pulled it off.

Better yet? I was able to isolate several frames to
get clear pics of attendees and perform a simple
reverse image search to separate "potential targets"
and "innocent bystanders".

It was something to start with anyhow.

I went back several times, as the hypno hang started
to be an every few weeks event. I would sit at the
same table to "get a drink" and collect my data.

I had a lot of files and information to sift through
but believe it or not - it actually paid off.

I got over a dozen leads from these simple drink and
observe days alone.

The added bonus was continuing to establish a
presence in the local kink community, building
rapport and putting my (slightly altered) face out
there- I mean that, and it was just fun.

I may have had a clear goal in mind, but that
certainly doesn't mean that my participation in the
scene was insincere. Much like, despite the info it
occasionally afforded me, my feelings and my
attraction to Spyder was none the less very sincere.

I'd been kinky for literally as long as I could
remember-a fact I warred against for a long time and
mostly kept under wraps for longer. Despite the
circumstances, it felt weirdly good to be open, even
if in an under wraps way, about "what" and who I
was... to explore an aspect of myself that I'd
fought for so long out of frustration for what it
seemed to bring into my life.

Predictably, it felt safer to be openly kinky in this
world than the mainstream. And oddly , I found the

people who I met mostly strengthened my (historically dangerously low) opinion of humanity.

This only increased my rage at the thought of any one of them being exploited by a predator in what SHOULD be a safe space. It was just so wrong- the idea of these "outsiders" (like me) finally feeling safe to be themselves, like they found a place to belong , and then being victimized within it.

It made me angry, but it also motivated me to do everything I could to cleanse the space of these assholes.

Back To The Web

A week or so more, and I was hopelessly back at
Spyder's lair - unbeknownst to him at the time, a 4
hour round trip.

In addition to the attraction to him and care for
him that still plagued me, I was also hoping that,
given his seniority in the scene, I could gleam some
useful information. Specifically, I was curious on
how deeply (if at all) O.D.O ran into the kink
scene, and if there was any tie to the illustrious
and mysterious I.C.O.M.

The evening was a pretty typical one, starting with
food of some kind in public space to a backdrop of
delightfully socially inappropriate conversation.

This was followed by arriving to his house and
getting chained again before imbibing several drinks
to numb the growing uncomfortably grey lines in my
life and my relationship... or whatever it was
...with Spyder, and the nerves at having both entered
the social scene and moved out of the city without
his knowledge. Naturally, this was eventually chased
with equally delightfully (consensually) rough play
with the sadist I might have accidentally started
falling for - seemingly against all sound logic and
reason.

After the sex part was over, he got up to use the
bathroom and check on his dogs, a rare occasion
where he left me unsupervised for a few precious
minutes in his abode. I decided to risk it. I
hadn't scanned the room for cameras, due - I suppose
- to fear they might be there and thus catch me

scanning and ruin everything. None-the-less, I
decided to risk a bit of snooping.

When I finally worked up the nerve, I carefully crept
out of bed and crouched down by the nightstand,
checking behind me to be sure he was still occupied
and, hearing no indicator of his return, for the 1st
time I took a peek under the massive oak framed bed
with the gothic headboard.

The robes had caught my eye first. When I pushed the
colorful fabrics aside, I saw the old box; it was
dust covered but intact. It was a shallow chest ,
shoved underneath silk robes of various colors and
questionable origin -similar to the one he insisted I
wear when exiting the bedroom (he liked me "draped in
silk"). I had just enough time to open the lid and
poke around, to catch a glimpse before I heard him
coming towards the door, thankfully he was halted
momentarily by the dog's knocking over a small vase.
I hurriedly closed the box and slid the robes back
into place. I hopped back into the bed and attempted
to slow down my heartrate, as the bedroom door
creaked open, and he popped his head in with a placid
smile, and a "Miss me?"

What I'd seen , what I'd seen made the blood drain
from my face and my extremities tremble. I had to
keep it together - I had to stay calm,

"Always-"

I replied simply, returning his smile.

I played it off but couldn't help worrying that he
suspected something. I willed my hands to stop
shaking as he grabbed them and forced my eyes to meet
his, now seemingly darker, pupils. I excused myself,
slipped on a silk robe and escaped to the bathroom. I

turned up the water faucet to cover my heaving over
the toilet.

"You ok? " he'd asked upon my return.

"Yeah , I'm sorry - I think the sushi didn't agree
with me tonight." I'd offer.

He seemed to buy it , if only somewhat suspiciously,
and we went to sleep. I'd made an excuse to leave
early the next morning , after our ceremonious coffee
and news time. He was the 1st guy since my ex to bring
me coffee in bed, and it meant much more to me than
is rational.

The box- the box was covered in a bunch of Mason
looking symbols , and full of small scrolls and
white silk tarnished with age. Each scroll appeared
to have a woman's name on it, and upon partially
unrolling one, I saw it contained measurements-
measurements of her entire body.

As I'd examined the scroll further, I'd noticed there
were 3 sheets that made up each. The first was the
list of measurements, the second was a filled-out
list of interests like the one he'd had me fill out,
and lastly, there was what appeared to be a contract.

I'd shakily but rapidly rolled the 3 papers back up
together, before I'd had to shove it back at the
sound of Spyder's return.

Coffee And Booze And Scary Questions

That afternoon, after the coffee and rapid exit from
Spyder's house, I took a mental health day. Wandering
to a local beachside bar, I ordered a very heavy pour
of very stiff red wine and gazed out at the pacific
ocean.

As I lowered the nearly empty wine glass, I was
filled with the most loathsome of quandary.

Spyder's odd lexicon of knock off Catholicism , his
readings on the occult, his eclectic collection of
books, his biker friend's mention of their having met
at "church", the oil he burned at that dinner that
was supposed to smell like a cathedral , his
ritualistic manner of domination, his obsession with
the Masons-

could he actually be involved in all this shit?!?

Everything felt haunted now... but most of all ,
THAT night , that night several months previous felt
haunting.

It was March. He'd invited me over, but not like
usually.

Usually, his idea of asking me out was asking, "what
you doing tonight?" while we were dancing and
waiting till I responded, "nothing much" before I
returned the question, at which point he'd shoot a
"sly" smile and respond "you " .

Charming, in some twisted way.

This time however, he'd invited me over a week in
advance and with a preconceived menu in mind .

It was to be a post St .Patty's Day feast; corned beef with rue, fingerling potatoes and roasted veggies.

He said he wanted me to meet his friends.

...

Do you ever think about how long it would take for someone , anyone, to notice you were gone?

...

I felt on edge leading up to the event, and the night of , I brought a couple of canned gin and tonics to calm my gut .

I started drinking immediately , as being left alone at a pop-up table between his 2 massive and- though friendly- also very intimidating friends had me a bit nervous.

He lit a strange looking incense burner in an oddly ceremonious manner before he put the food down in front of us all. He told me a friend of his made blends and this one was "supposed to smell like a church".

It seemed like we rushed thru dinner, which I thought was the point of this little meeting . Something tightened in my gut.

Before I knew it , they were both saying their goodbyes and heading out for the night. Spyder said we were going for a quick ride- no need to take anything. I slid my phone in my back pocket when he wasn't looking but left my purse. It was dark outside and unusually gusty.

After driving around for maybe half an hour, he
pulled to a stop beside some old warehouses in the
historic district of town. There was no one around ,
and the wind cut through the alleys all the harder. I
was trying to figure out where we were, and why we
were there, when he started talking.

He shared a genuinely heartbreaking story about
leaving Catholicism, about being betrayed by people
and turning to poly and discovering kink.

It was the first time he'd opened up to me like that.
I was touched, but also a bit anxious given our
surroundings. Suddenly his eyes went from glassy to
black again as he said , "I always promised myself
I wouldn't ever date someone I couldn't share-" and
he stared past me with an unsettling levity.

"Wait, what ?" I felt myself recoil backwards
towards the door. Yeah, he was poly, but did
"share" have a more sinister implication in this
instance? This unrest was only amplified by his next
statement -which echoed his apparent feeling that if
he were to push past my pre-discussed boundaries and
I "didn't stop him" in the act than it was "my
fault" not his for what happened.

The air grew heavy around us as he seemed to be
struggling with or deciding on - something.

He started talking again, I don't remember about
what. I felt the confusing feeling.

Looking around at the dark street we were parked on,
I saw we were near railroad tracks beside an old
building I'd never seen. It had a red door and very
much resembled a creepy, white barn. The streets were
completely empty and a single weathered streetlight
cast everything in an eerie sallow hue. The outlines

of massive sycamore trees blew in the gust of wind that howled down the alley nearby.

I interrupted , " No Spyder, the entire reason we pre-discuss boundaries in agonizing detail is so you DO NOT push past them , not so you can walk all over them and then blame me after for not "speaking up" or "for letting it happen" while I'm in sub-space . Then, while willing myself to sound calm, as I figured anything resembling fear would be blood in the water for a sadist, I continued; "Where are we Spyder? ... and why did you bring me here?".

He seemed to snap out of it, or maybe realize I had?

He also seemed to be deciding something. I don't know why, but after a moment of silence filled only with the feeling without a name and staring into his suddenly emotionless face, he seemed to make up his mind about something- and without another word, he drove us back to his house.

I felt like that night meant something- but was it a near brush with something sinister? Or merely our first brush with something equally terrifying: "intimacy".

Could all these little things be a coincidence?? Was my trauma and my passionate (to the level of somewhat obsessive) research clouding my logic... ` making everything look more sinister than it really was?

After all , I already knew he loved silk (as did I). He'd always been open about being interested in the Masons, even sharing that he had family members who had been high ranking members. The measurements were, creepy... undeniably so, but maybe it was just an offbeat practice , him playing with an "ownership" fetish in a mostly harmless, though thoroughly off-putting, way .

It could all easily be explained away, really.

Or, my inner cynic retorted, were my growing feelings- my love- my power dynamic with this man blinding me to the obvious danger I was in... whether it involved ICOM or not? As it could all equally paint a picture of a rather sinister situation.

He had once said if I looked long enough, I'd find something I "wouldn't like" , that he'd "beg my forgiveness". Was this it? Was there something even worse??

I guess it's just that , once you see a certain amount of evil, it's hard not to see it everywhere, but is this fact really _trauma tainting one's reality_? Or is it merely _experience opening one's eyes_ to what most people can't stomach seeing, will never have too??

Because, equally, BEFORE you see a certain amount of evil, you tend to be blind to it, even when it's right under your nose.

Where's the line, the line between learning from experience and letting it poison everything you see?

There's so much nuance in life, in people... yet there are undoubtedly some situations that require no real consideration of said nuance, that supersede nuance.

The fact was, regardless of whether he was involved in something deeper or related to my research, the control tendencies - the slant towards slave/master dynamics and sadism - that was dangerous enough.

Where Are You?

Spyder's incoming text snapped me out of my buzz and deeply disturbing contemplations.

"Where are you?" he asked. I felt disturbingly sure he already had a vague idea. I hadn't told him that I'd moved out of the city, just that I' moved houses and was keeping a low profile.

Was it my imagination, or did he grow eerily silent as I slid open the first door, and made my way up the stairs as we talked?

"Oh, you live on an upper floor I see-" he taunted. My stomach dropped. No, apparently, I wasn't imagining it.

"You know, I went on a bike ride the other day, I thought it'd be funny if I ran into you... I've been keeping track of where I go ... what neighborhoods I cover. I haven't found you- yet."

I'd fucked up in mentioning that I had a claw foot tub (I was excited, ok?), without considering how much this little factoid would narrow my possible dwelling in the city we'd shared-

or that he was acutely aware of this , given his 45 years living in the city AND a large part of his job revolving around architecture and being intimately familiar with construction in the area.

Not to worry, he made sure to remind me of these facts and point out my error- with obvious Machiavellian glee.

Fuck, I hate sadists...

but, I mean, I also seem to fall in love with them historically.
Oh dysfunction, how familiar you have become.

There was only really one neighborhood, in midtown, that fit the description of an old apartment with no air and a clawfoot tub- the one he volunteered that he'd been taking his impromptu bike rides through.

Thanks to all these - now mutually understood factors- he had figured out that I was probably in an outlying area rather than in the city proper, and -you guessed it- he told me so.

Thankfully, even he didn't guess how much effort I was willing to put in to get away , how far I'd ACTUALLY moved, or how good my poker face is when it's needed.

I knew it was risky- potentially even deranged -to think I could keep investigating, while seeing him, being in his arms, and lying about something as big as moving to another city.

It was almost as deranged as thinking I could keep the door of communication open with him, without inviting potentially fatal disaster.

I tried to not allow what I'd seen under Spyder's bed to affect how I acted around him, but it was (obviously) still on my mind. What possible explanation could there be for all those scrolls? The contracts??

Was it an "innocent" albeit somewhat icky trophy chest of sorts? Or was it something more sinister? Would he tell me if I asked?

Did I want him to?

I wasn't sure if he'd figured out what I'd seen, or what he'd do if he did.

Whether related or not, in the following weeks, his intensity with me took a swift trajectory upwards both in physical severity and aspects of control.

That Bruised Feeling

Looking in the mirror, I felt unexpectedly sick. It was only a few bruises, a couple of mouth shaped ones dramatically visible, and peeking out even with my shirt on.

He hadn't done anything I didn't enjoy in order to make them appear, but they still filled me with an odd sadness that I didn't understand. I guess it just kind of looked like I'd been beat up, the way they were placed.

He tried to say they were "pretty" like he always did with the marks, but these- for whatever reason -felt distinctly unpretty, sad, to me. Maybe it had to do with coming from the history I had, where marks hadn't always been consensually or playfully crafted. Maybe it had to do with his recent unsettling trend towards voicing the desire to incorporate striking as a part of our sex life... and his seeming disappointment and surprise that I was standing firm on my "no closed fist" hard line.

Perhaps it was mostly that he had been fully informed of the former, yet still advocated for the latter- well that and the sensation that his idea of a "scene" was seeming more and more like his just doing what he wanted when he wanted than an actual not only pre-discussed but adequately planned scene. "If sex is a roadmap, then I'm not interested," he flatly stated more than once when I'd attempt to explain the importance of context, full ongoing consent and compartmentalization in distinguishing a consensually "violent" scene and flat out violence.

It's arguable that given some scene members concept of 24/7 and CNC, and his seeming lack of 1st hand experience in the level of trauma and PTSD I was dealing with could have played a role. Regardless, the effect was the same.

Still, he had never actually forced anything, and he could be so supportive sometimes... sweet even. So, despite my horror at his seeming callous insensitivity, I continued to explain things like functional empathy and the vulnerability of a sub in a power dynamic to a man in his 40's.

As for the bruises, given my feelings (whether "rational" or not) and the looks I got from men on the street when I was alone and sporting them, I requested Spyder avoid marking that area for the time being at least.

I requested...

I requested another person not bruise my body.

Anyhow-

He replied that he would be sure in the future to "let me know" if "we" were going to do that before he marked them.

"DID I FUCKING STUTTER ?" I thought.

"I said I don't want that to happen, not that I want notice-" I restated aloud, feeling my blood pressure rising by the second, and attempting to will myself not to scream or start tearing up, "- and WE aren't doing anything, you are... and I want it to stop ."

I knew the last bit came out angry, I WAS angry, trauma brain continued my internal dialogue out loud, "It's my body... MY BODY... I said NO, NO means NO ... Ok?? NO." I tried to stop it, but it

was too late, I'd said it; " My body", not his ...
MINE.

I knew I'd pay for it, but the damage was already
done... and frankly, I wasn't sorry. I couldn't
fucking take it anymore. I wanted out. Perhaps both
his interest in marking me at (his)will, and my
compulsion to assert ownership over my own body was
partially due to another recent disagreement.

I got a tattoo.

It wasn't anything crazy , but I had the "gall" to
get it without his "permission" , without
"consulting" him -and he lost his shit when he saw
it.

When he found out the artist was male, the outrage
increased significantly.

I was shocked at his reaction at first, and then
equally outraged.

He had insisted on my absence from his home until it
healed, and then when he did see me, I could tell by
the way he stared at it that this was far from a
closed issue for him.

His overall interest in striking me, seemed to
skyrocket after these incidents.

Just for the record, it wasn't actually the
suggestion of slapping me in the face that bothered
me. It was something in the way he expressed that
want, the despise that laced his eyes when he said
it... the timing and the conjunction with a sudden
renewed interest in the kind of sex that *used to be*
fun with him.

It used to be fun because we'd joke about "hate sex"
... there was never actually palpable hate , or
anything past mild irritation, passion . But now ,
now I could not only see it but also feel it. It
wasn't fun anymore because this time, I could feel
that it wasn't a joke.

He hated me, it felt like he ACTUALLY hated me. It
wasn't sex anymore, it was actual punishment, and it
made me feel dead inside. It felt like his whole body
was screaming to-inside of- my body; "I HATE you."

Did he realize any of this? Was it even conscious? I
truly don't know, but regardless the result was the
same.

I started trying to avoid sex with him, and oddly ,
he seemed to want it more. It'd be easy to assume
this was due to some sadistic component, but perhaps
this effect was merely his sensing that I was pulling
away, and a natural response to try to grasp what
was starting to slip through his fingers.

Regardless, I started crying when it happened, and he
didn't seem to mind.

In fact, he told me that tears turned him on.
Arousal via tears is - apparently- far from an
unheard-of phenomenon. It's actually known as
"Dacryphilia". Still, I was horrified -obviously-
when he told me.

Then again, it would be easy to assume someone who's
turned on by tears is a literal monster, that they
are enjoying the grieving, the pain of another -
however, it's equally possible that they are merely
turned on by the emotional intimacy and
vulnerability that's exhibited in an act as intimate
as tears. Where's the line in where these two meet?

Wouldn't the knowledge of hurt preclude arousal in any feeling individual?

I don't know. I'm starting to think that some people are just wired differently ... that he was wired differently. That maybe there was just more divisions and compartmentalization's in his brain than was "typical". And no one can help their brain makeup. Still, everyone is responsible for their actions and how they affect others. It allowed me to have empathy for him. I felt empathy for him that he seemed to struggle with functional empathy for me.

I think he tried, but it just wasn't enough.

He tried to fight his nature to some extent ... but maybe that line was just too hard to mark from a first-person perspective. I believe he was probably as sincere as he was capable of.

I respected that he tried. I hated that it failed, but I knew at some level that it was all for the best.

He tried, in his own way and I didn't - I actually still don't - want him to feel bad.

It wasn't enough. It still hurt.

It was still fucked up,

and I won't apologize for recognizing that either .

I reached my breaking point; I knew I couldn't bear to keep sleeping with him ... I just couldn't.

Were all the little things calculated cruelty or callous carelessness?

Did the distinction really fucking matter?

I was fascinated by him at first, primarily because of all of the above and the seeming contradictions it produced . Perhaps I wanted to understand him so badly, that I overlooked the obvious.

The "why" is fascinating in a twisted way perhaps, but ultimately meaningless in terms of appropriate reaction, of appropriate action.

At the end of the day, who gives a shit why he's being mean or perpetually complicating your life - or if he is "trying" or if you care about him; you just have to get out. You owe it to yourself to get out, to have a chance at being actually happy, to have a chance at peace.

The Breaking

He was calm , upset but calm , when I told him thru
the phone. I wasn't trying to be cruel , I just knew
I'd never be able to do it in person. Also, frankly,
after what I'd seen under the bed, I was a bit
worried about what he may do.

"I'm sorry, I just can't ..."

And it was true, I had felt something , and that
made being with him while continuing any form of
research far too dangerous.

I just needed to get my head straight, to get to the
bottom of this mystery without putting him in any
danger and without putting myself in any further
potential danger with him.

I made it about poly and monogamy , which was
partially true- I reminded him that I'd already told
him I wasn't poly but I was open to an open, casual
relationship - which he had of course wasted no time
in pushing way too close and way far past any and
all emotional boundaries to work.

I added that, in all fairness, I didn't exactly stop
him. We clicked on so many levels, and he had the
intoxicating combination of (at least some)
emotional intelligence, listening skills and being a
near perfect other half to my twisted sexual
tendencies. So, it was somewhat hopeless to try to
slow it down.

We were both fire, and he was a bit of an arsonist.

At which point, he -astonishingly- suggested
attempting monogamy.

I reminded him that monogamy seemed highly complicated to switch to and required more faith in humanity than I currently possessed.

I didn't mention the other thought running through my head, which was that monogamy also went completely against my research project and any attempt to stay objective and compartmentalize. I also didn't mention aloud that I highly suspected his already (very) present control issues would likely skyrocket in a one-on-one arrangement. Nor did I mention my growing fears of his potential involvement in O.D.O. or I.C.O.M. or something equally sinister- given his connections, slants towards complete "ownership", or the little box of horrors I'd recently found tucked under his bed.

I added (out loud) that there was also the sinking feeling that if we did manage to pull off full monogamy together, neither of us would be happy in it together long term.

I told him we were too addicted to each other to stay poly, equally though, we were too fire and too differing in our wants and views to be monogamous.

I told him tortured lovers it seemed would always be our fate... and I was no sadist, I didn't want to torture either of us.

I didn't tell him that- after my daring to get a tattoo and banning boob bruises- it was becoming increasingly obvious I would just be punished until he was done with me, and I didn't want to be punished anymore.

I had to end it.

After a moment of silence, he took me by surprise:

"You found the scrolls, huh?" He asked with playful anger. Then he let the question linger, as I tried to catch my breath again.

"I wasn't trying to- I mean, I wasn't..." what was I going to say ? That I wasn't snooping?? I mean I undeniably was- but was that REALLY the issue at this point??

"Yes." I finally answered

He continued, "Honey, I told you that you'd find things you didn't want to if you looked hard enough, haha. Please don't tell me that's why you're running away from me ?"

"What the fuck Spyder? This isn't funny, what were those??" I spat out with a tremble.

"I mean you saw what they are I assume, measurements, contracts, info sheets..." the casual almost amused tone of his voice was both unsettling and utterly infuriating.

"What , from your exes-"

"-Formers" he interrupted.

"-whatever," I continued, " Is that what it is? A huge box of trophies of your 'formers' under where we sleep? Is that what I am to you ? Just another scroll for your box??" I was shaking.

"Whoa, whoa- don't put words in my mouth-" he started with that patronizing tone that made me blindly livid before continuing, " It's not what you think and no, you are much more than a trophy to me." he offered.

"Wow, ok , so I am a trophy but also 'other stuff'?" I responded bitterly, "-and what do you mean 'it's not what I think' ? Then what the hell is it??" I demanded, "-because you said you loved me. You talked about a future with me... is that what you told everyone in the box?? Is that the 'future' you spoke of... auctioning me off like one of your 'former' slaves??"

"They were SUBS" he interjected.

"That's fucking bullshit... you can call it whatever the fuck you want to make it less 'scary' more 'palatable', but you don't auction off subs, you don't 'own' subs, that is SLAVE shit -okay?- SLAVE,"

"Let me talk! OK? " He shot back. " I'll tell you, but you have to calm down, and listen."

"Ok" I responded in the calmest voice I could muster.

"I told you I teach classes sometimes on kink -" he started.

"yeah..." I shrugged.

"Well, I'm also a trainer, a teacher of sorts... those were formers but not all MY subs, you could think of those scrolls as my students, my projects." He offered.

"I'm sorry, what? So where are they?" I demanded.

"Some of them decided a certain path wasn't for them- it sounds like similar to yourself- the others , when they were ready, I introduced them to my community, my church. Depending on their sheets, sometimes they'd do various service and sometimes participate in the auction, or I'd trade or sell them to other Dom's-" he stated flatly.

"'Similar to myself'?? Wait , are you fucking serious?? So, in your mind, are you my 'teacher'? Do you think you're 'training' me for something?? " I shot back.

"Nothing you wouldn't like, nothing you wouldn't want." He offered casually.

"How THE FUCK do you know what I want?? Fuck, how arrogant are you?!?

And church? What are you talking about? You said you were agnostic..." I trailed off,

suddenly feeling disturbingly sure of _exactly_ what he meant.

"Well, I believe in service, community, kink, sex-" he started dramatically.

"Sex, kink - they're great , but they're not a fucking religion..." I interrupted.

"That's your opinion." He responded, irritated.

"Is it though??- I offered, " This is deranged. So, it's your opinion that it's ethical to sell human beings , to trade them like cattle? "

"They weren't forced to do anything. " He offered back.

"Maybe not physically, maybe not literally- but that doesn't mean you get off scot-free from having any responsibility for their wellbeing -" I responded.

"They made their own choices; I just showed them the way. it's not on me," he asserted.

"Their own choices? After how much gas lighting and manipulation? After how many declarations of 'love' that ended with their essence being reduced to a rolled-up scrap in an old box??

Was it their choice to go past the line willingly, Spyder ? Or their 'choice' not to stop you when YOU, after your charms, crossed the line knowingly?" I demanded.

"What's the difference?" he said with a scoff.

"I think we're done here." I replied with disgust.

"If you have to paint me as a monster to move on-" He started bitterly.

"Don't flatter yourself. You can definitely be an asshole, but I don't think you're a monster. I've met monsters. You're just a sadist with a god complex. " I shot back.

He laughed from his stomach, the way he always did when I said something too close to true, "Well, I'm sorry you feel that way. Best of luck to you." He offered.

"Genuine apologies as usual I see..." I observed with a shake of my head and a sigh, but continued, "Look, regardless of 'what' you are , what else you've done, or why you did it-" I paused for a deep breath to put out the fire in my diaphragm before continuing,

"-thank you Spyder, I'll never forget what you did for me... and best of luck to you also."

I'm not sure who hung up 1st, but there was a sense of closure at least, of some strange intangible mutual (almost) respect, despite our wildly different views, and the reprehensible nature of some of his practices and statements.

And it was true, I did appreciate what Spyder had (allegedly) done for me when no one else would.

I cried tears in the privacy of my own home that night, with no one there to fetishize them, and then I moved on the best that I could.

I changed my burner number and device and real number for good measure.

Though, given his nature, I felt reasonably confident he wouldn't try to find me once it was over. His whole draw to domination was built on the concept of his target coming to him, choosing freely to be possessed. It would be "beneath" him to stalk or harass; it would defeat the whole "point" if he had to force it.

I couldn't help the care I'd felt for him. There were parts of him that seemed kind, like there was hope for him - for "us". I'd learned what I could and gotten far too close to comfortable with someone potentially far too close to the very dangerous subject that I was investigating.

Was he involved in this shit? Were my "feelings" merely the effects of a skilled and seasoned manipulator on a subby empath with no sense of normalcy?

Perhaps?

Perhaps not completely...

Perhaps not at all,

but I couldn't risk it.

Was "it" deeper feelings than I wanted, continuing
down a dangerously controlling path, or getting
close to someone potentially involved in what I was
researching?

Who's to say,

but I couldn't risk "it",

not in the middle of what I was in.

There was one thing for sure-whether he was for real
or not - I had loved him.

Now, the love turned to pain and eventually to numb.

Soon, I felt nothing at all, which seemed like a
safer place to be for the time being .

A Pretty Insanely Unadvisable Idea

Once I'd had a day to process with a clearer head, it seemed pretty obvious from what had passed between us, that Spyder really WAS in this O.D.O. business. And it would seem he was an at least occasionally active member of MASU and The Association.

But I still felt strangely sure that there was no way he was involved with I.C.O.M. His whole philosophy was built on participants going willingly- perhaps under heavy manipulation and grooming -but still justifiably "willingly" in his own mind. Then again, overconfidence in one's assumptions- however grounded in reason- can lead to tragedy if not checked with frequent safeguards and cynicism. Plus, people can justify a lot of crazy shit in their head. So, I decided to leave the question of Spyder's involvement in I.C.O.M., as just that, a question.

Now monetarily, back to the sketchy Dom from that play party. He did come thru with some useful info and a few additional events I didn't yet know about. We were supposed to meet at one such suspension event a couple hours south, when he ended up having to cancel at the last minute.

He had purchased the tickets , so he had to give me the name he purchased them under so I could get in.

That's how I found out his actual scene name, or at least his social handle- which turned out to be "MindTopper" , real subtle bro. I played dumb, and thanks to his aforementioned tendency to underestimate nearly everyone other than himself- he bought it.

I attended the aforementioned suspension and ropes jam without him and met two characters of a similar caliber in the back "experienced" area. I overheard one of them expounding to the other on the merits of utilizing breathwork on a sub before roping her up. I willed myself to resist an eye roll. Once the clearly less experienced one approached me (because, of course he did), I learned a few more useful tidbits. After dropping a few names of play spaces and meetups, he mentioned a couple of his own, including an upcoming kink conference of sorts that was to span several days and be held at a well-known high rise hotel south of the city in a month or so. I told him I hadn't decided if I was going yet or not and gave him my burner number in case.

Once I got home, I did a bit more research on this event. Though tempting, most of me felt like going would be too risky, kinksters from all over the country would be attending, and I couldn't risk getting recognized by the wrong person or tranced again in a setting where I was vastly outnumbered. It was a useful tip regardless. Like so many other events and spaces in this world , I never would have found the info on it online if I didn't know exactly what to search for, but since I did, it was absurdly simple to find all the deets I could hope for.

First of all, there was a huge number of the guest presenters that were doing workshops on hypno kink or sex magik related topics- even the event photographer had a hypnokink related scene name. There were speakers scheduled to attend from all over the country.

In the line-up of truly questionable presenters, I saw a familiar name, a familiar face;

Osbourn Black.

His about me section, no doubt self-penned, described
him as a kinkster, a warlock -

and a member of O.D.O.

Though I'd suspected it, this was more evidence of
what I'd feared. I felt surer than ever, that he was
hunting for fresh meat in the local scene under the
guise of "education".

So, after some playing around with the destructive
idea of using myself as bait, I reluctantly accepted
that for it to fully "work", or at least for me to
get anything recorded, I'd need to meet them outside
of the scene... preferably in private. This was not
only incredibly dangerous for my sanity and my cover
but could easily lead to my unfortunate demise and
would, by its very nature, require me to accept the
potential of being further victimized via violation
of mind and body.

Plus, how could I be sure it wouldn't "work" so well
that I lost myself, my mission? How long could I
last, until the very real tendencies that made me
"believable", made me too vulnerable to be worth the
risk?

Mindtopper had mentioned that if I did want to go
the conference, I should let him know, that maybe we
could meet up at his place for a bit before, as he
lived nearby the hotel.

After inching up to the precipice of this wildly
unadvisable idea, I decided to pause and stare into
the abyss that lay before me, to count the costs, to
weigh the risks and possible reward.

Was it really worth the risk, the risk of losing
everything... of losing myself?

And perhaps more pressing in my mind, if they took me
out , if I walked myself into my own death - who
would be left to (attempt to) take these assholes
out? It was just me, I didn't have a team or even
backup; it was just me.

I turned down the invite.

Just In Case...

Do you ever think about how long it would take for someone - anyone- to notice you were gone? Or look for you?

Or who exactly it would be who did, bother to look... who it'd be who'd noticed ...

If you, say, died or disappeared, or got taken?

I do,

a lot recently. I find my mind wandering to this subject in a disturbingly frequent and somewhat fixated manner as of late.

So much so, that -after contemplating using myself as human bait for sadistic predators- I decided to create a little bundle to help placate this concerning preoccupying hypothetical.

I scribbled down any pertinent info I could think of , my research and my affairs- should they need to be put in order. This included, of course, directions for my Viking funeral -assuming they had a body I mean.

Though I suppose a flotation device aflame with memorabilia would do in a pinch... and probably be more legal than a burning corpse in public waterways.

Also? There was to be passion flowers, dahlias, Gerber daisies, sage... plenty of good blues and grunge rock, libations of cava and sangria, dancing and merriment. I wanted an angel rubber ducky on my grave/ memorial area. I left directions on how to divide my meager possessions and lastly, but

certainly not least, I left a shit list for anyone
who felt motivated to "take care of" it.

I folded the crumpled notebook sheets into a manilla
envelope, and sealed it with a thick layer of masking
tape- but not before scrawling an inscription onto
the front of it ; "In case of ---"

I paused , "in case of what?"

Well, I wasn't quite sure; I wasn't even clear what
to be afraid of yet.

I felt too much rage to fully register fear, I think.

Still, I knew enough to be strategically cautious.

"In case of disappearance, disembowelment, apparent
insanity or any other such emergency "
There, at least if I'm taken or murdered (or both),
my friends can chuckle at my dark humor while they
search for my remains.

"What friends ?" my dark(er) inner cynic retorted
with a snort.

She wasn't wrong-

  the fact that I say "she" probably makes that
blindingly apparent.

I hadn't exactly let a lot of people in recently-
then again- it hadn't *exactly* gone well when I'd
tried in the past.

Plus, hunting an underground ring of sadistic
hypnotists makes for neither pleasant nor advisable
dinner conversations.

How do I know -besides perhaps the intuitive social
norms I seem to keep violating with reckless abandon?

Funny you should ask.

I'm Off To See The ----

He had a massive almost Gandolf beard, which would
give his later confounding insistence that he was a
"wizard" a tinge of comic relief.

I was new in town and attempting some momentary
reprieve from the utter torment of my own mind via
popping out for a drink one Thursday evening. I
picked a bar that promised to be the perfect sweet
spot between dive and cocktail bar. You know the
type: low lights, purse hooks under the bar, grunge
rock, fresh bar garnish, strong pours, and solid
bartenders who could nail a negroni with their eyes
closed - but who still didn't have man buns or call
themselves "mixologists".

It was packed, and I was (almost) the only single
person there- which served as just another great
reminder of the growing likelihood of dying alone.

But I spied one other person in a potentially more
awkward situation than me. There was a bearded fellow
, sharply dressed and sipping an old fashion that
nicely highlighted the strange hand tattoo I caught
a glimpse of as he took a sip. He was a third wheel
(or a third?) to an eccentric couple sitting to my
right. I decided fuck it and struck up a
conversation with all of them - internally patting
myself on the back for the great strides in "being
more social" I was making.

I left with a light buzz and his number, and

 texted him goodnight before I passed out.

...

A few days later , he texted me asking if I'd like to grab dinner downtown, and I agreed.

For a few lovely weeks, I thought I may have actually met a "normal" person in "real life" and potentially have inadvertently freed myself from the tiresome and admittedly insanely risky world of online dating. He opened doors, planned dates, and seemed genuinely interested in me.

Better yet? He seemed to have a brain. Grant it, I was having difficulty in developing a sexual interest in him - which is definitely a necessary part of a sexual relationship- but I suppose I'd been thru enough psychopaths to give it the good old college try anyhow.

Besides the mostly absent physical attraction (save his interesting tattoos and sharp choices of clothing), there was also his apparent lack of personal hygiene in the form of things like showering or deodorant. As our interaction continued, I also found us to be very incompatible in the sexual department. He was the type to insist on unnecessarily emotionally intimate behavior that I would have preferred to hold off on, or- better yet- completely avoid entirely .

Before long, he was asking me to date him , and I surprised myself in- despite everything- actually somewhat considering it. I felt the need for some reason, to give a few disclaimers before either of us continued this line of consideration, in hindsight perhaps to dissuade him from continuing his interest. What , you ask , did this include ? Oh, just vague allusion to hypnotists, and as a side topic the "crazy" local Drowley cult I'd just found out about.

Imagine my surprise, when instead of shock or disgust at the latter bit, he merely replied calmly, "Oh yeah , I know about them , I go to Temple Dophia".

"I'm sorry , wait , what??" I stumbled back, internally reprimanding my own stupidity.

He went on to inform me that his "temple" was a spinoff of sorts to the greater body of O.D.O., and that he went there for "Gnostic Mass" regularly.

It was late, and I wasn't ready to ask more questions that night, so I said good night with promises to brunch and discuss in the morning.

The following day , we did brunch, but he did all the talking. In fact, it seemed he enjoyed the sound of his own voice so much that I didn't even really need to be there at all . He was going on (and on ... and on...) about being "gnostic" and how he was - wait for it- A WIZARD. Upon my "I'm sorry , wait , what??" he insisted that wizard just meant "wise man" - a sentiment nearly as ludicrous in this context.

While he was enamored at his own self-indulgent ramblings, I got a better look at that hand tattoo that had caught my eye to begin with. I managed to interrupt him, to ask about the meaning behind the faintly familiar looking symbol on his hand. It was a woman with many arms, and just as he started to explain - I remembered where I'd seen this imagery. It was a symbol I'd run across in my research. I was beginning to realize that he was perhaps much more involved in this Temple Dophia than he'd led me to believe.

"Fuck".

I also managed to get out of him what this
mysterious "gnostic mass" really consisted of. I sat
in stunned silence, as he casually mentioned a "high
priestess" coming out naked , and basically an orgy
full of strangers drinking wine and pretending they
were in a "spiritual" place- instead of , well , an
orgy full of horny strangers.

I struggled to get words out, but when I did it came
out something like " I've got to go; I need to
go..." .

"I love you " he blurted out.

For the love of fuck-really, again?? But this time
there was definitely no hint of any kind of
reciprocation, no matter what type of semantics
employed.

"I just met you ... I'm sorry , but you don't know
me enough to love me . I'm sorry ... this just isn't
going to work for me . I wish you the best, only the
best. Please don't call me . Good bye ." I stammered
and hurried out of the café.

About a week later he sent me a picture of an
incredibly long "love" letter he'd written me , which
he also insisted on reading me via a very late drunk
call I only answered to attempt to smooth things
over enough to lessen the chances of him showing up
to murder me. He seemed nearly moved to tears by his
own flowery monologue, which actually did help
lessen my guilt at hanging up swiftly after telling
him to please move on .

He didn't , of course. He continue to thread bare the
last fucking shreds of my nerves over the next couple
of MONTHS via randomly sending me nonsensical yet
strangely menacing feeling texts such as ; " I'm not

a bad person" , " there are monsters in the dark I think ", " you'll see I am a wizard " ... and so forth.

Because, I really needed another reason to look over my fucking shoulder constantly.

On the bright side, I'd gotten a few names from him, and despite the uncomfortably personal nature of it all and the need to change my number for the umpteenth time- I was that much closer to putting the pieces of this odd (and growingly odder) mystery together.

It was definitely becoming obvious that this group had very different crowds at different levels. The mass that the wizard spoke of was (it turns out) - unlike any of the cult's other meetings- open to the public. Could this base, public facing level be used -whether "sinister" or not- to sniff out promising recruits to more secretive levels, to proper initiation? Could a few extra bad eggs also be using it to recruit both victims and perpetrators for something darker and more exclusive? Even I.C.O.M. itself?

Phase 3: The Most-est Dangerous Game

After researching the names from the Wizard and coming up mostly empty handed, I started wondering, what if this mess- this puzzle- is less like interweaving strings and more like a Ven diagram?

Perhaps my own trauma had been blurring the more nuanced explanation of how all these threads interrelated and to what extent.

Having had a bit more time to process, having researched a bit more- I wondered: what if O.D.O. , MaSU (as questionable as they were) had nothing to do with I.C.O.M. or the hypnofucks. What if one person, maybe a few bad apples in O.D.O. were syphoning people from Gnostic masses , perhaps other places like some of the kink meet ups , maybe even the general public with help from a select few of these hypnofucks - and then delivering them to I.C.O.M.? That would actually make way more sense. Something as secretive as I.C.O.M. probably wouldn't risk being directly associated with a more public facing cult, but if a handful- or even one- member could use their standing in O.D.O. as a front- as a hunting ground- that would be plausible.

I'd been quite the busy little bitch after the breakup, teaching myself the ropes of the digital universe, using those ropes to slowly encircle a list of individuals connected to my targets , then my actual targets.

Now I was starting to slowly tighten said rope, with the end goal of eventually strangling the life out of said targets , before they even knew what had them rigged-

figuratively speaking, of course.

I braced myself against the wall, gripping the edges of my little blue laptop as I pressed enter.

This was soo beyond questionable, but I didn't know how else to get in without involving another innocent party so Cie la vie.

The video I'd just offered up as "proof" that I belonged in this deranged discord chat room was of a woman seemingly entranced , naked and being subjected to a myriad of utterly deplorable things...

The woman pictured,

was also me.

The video is one I'd created with the explicit purpose of using it as bait for the sick fucks I'm hunting.

Thankfully , they don't much care if the video is primarily the afflicted party and with a bit of editing, knowledge of deep fake techniques and studying their preferences , I'd made a convincingly authentic little mashup.

Obviously having first hand experience with what this shit is actually like, went a long way in making it appear to be the real deal , so thanks Fuckface for that bit of knowledge.

"Got ya!"

I pounded the air in excitement, as the messages started pouring in - many using the same or similar usernames as they did on other sites I'd already linked them to Fuckface thru.

"Oh, you've seen this girl in several others ? She's a fun time huh?

Fuck these bastards... die slowly pricks, slowly..."
I ranted angrily aloud, to no one but my fluffy cat
who eyed me with irritation from her bed by my desk.

I took a brief interlude in my spacious and
conveniently quite soundproof closet, to smash a few
more wine bottles in garbage bags with a hammer-a
recently discovered "alternative" therapy for my ever
growing rage.

This was gonna take more booze than I thought to get
through, but I was far too pissed off to be deterred.

Eventually, after much conversation with oxygen
bandits who "shared" things that made me want to
wash my computer in bleach (and possibly spike their
drinks with a splash also), I had developed enough
artificial repour (read falsified confirmation
bias) to ask for what I had been after for years.

I cautiously threw out that I had an "interest" in
more videos specifically with the woman from my own
video -that I thought it might be "funny" to watch
what had made her "so much fun for me".

The moments seemed like hours as the "typing" dots
appeared under the username badgerwarefare91.

Getting what you asked for is a mixed bag. As the
file loaded in the DM section of my chat- I saw a
still image that made my guts drop lower than I
thought possible. I couldn't breathe- for a second,
I couldn't breathe.

I was staring at an image of myself, but I had no
direct recollection of what was happening.

Fuckface was there, no surprise, but so was someone
else.

Suddenly, it came to the surface-the vomit I was suppressing that is.

After a brief interlude hovering over a toilet and screaming, I was able to pull myself together enough to take a shot of gin and respond.

" This looks deliciously vile- how could I get my hands on the full length feature?"

These pricks psycho babble was wayyy to easy to hack.

More dots followed,

then stopped,

then started again.

Just when I worried he may have changed his mind, I got an invite to another sever-a more exclusive one it would seem. There was also a link to a folder within it labeled "Virtuosos".

I took a deep breath and clicked open, but I wasn't ready for what I found .

There were dozens of videos of me alone. God only knows how many others they'd done this to. Without going into the additional aforementioned psycho babble it was necessary to engage in to get the info I did , or exactly how many hours I spent establishing a false creeper identity and building both an online dark web presence and the "rapport" needed- I got more than I'd hoped for my efforts.

As it turned out, it seems these guys were effectively trading trigger words- ones they'd established to initiate trance in susceptible individuals - and addresses of the associated victims, for bitcoin.

It was a whole other level of sex trafficking. One that was virtually untraceable, and operating completely under the radar. They didn't have to physically store or transport the victims to the buyers; they only had to maintain post hypnotic suggestion and location data on each previously tranced victim.

This was so much bigger than I'd originally thought, and I was beyond "in over my head".

So, naturally , I decided to dig a bit deeper in ... double down on my already totally fucked position.

Fun Fact:

Did you know that you can still write to inmates? Crazy, right? And narcissistic ones with nothing better to do than wait to die, sure are fucking eager to chat about their illusions of grander, enough to give illustrious details about some pretty juicy info that would usually get someone murdered... if they weren't already scheduled to die I mean,

or so I hear.

Okay, yeah-

so I *may have* started writing a serial killer,

but not just any serial killer.

Yep, bingo! You guessed it; a certain waste of flesh that had ties to I.C.O.M.

I posed as a huge "fan" (gag), and obviously was cautious in using a fake identity also.

As ego is the simplest way to crack a psychopath, it wasn't actually even that hard to get him to "open up".

Once he was comfortable, and I truly felt I needed a fucking shower from wading around in the utter filth of this creep's mind, I pushed a little more and asked him a few more detailed questions about I.C.O.M. I figured, as he was in California also, perhaps he had former or current knowledge about how they found their victims in the golden state.

I'd have to approach it just the right way, not too
eager or he'd be spooked but not too disinterested or
his ego wouldn't bite.

After some back and forth , I got the confirmation I
was looking for: I.C.O.M. was- in fact- scraping
victims from public BDSM scenes and had -true to
form- secured several members in notable positions in
the largest ones. Also, many members of I.C.O.M. were
also involved with a notable cult - and utilized the
more public facing events as a preying ground both
for potential members and victims. He never directly
named the cult, but quoted it's founder's motto as a
subtle but not so subtle hint.

When I mentioned that some of my "friends" were into
covert trancing , he laughed and added that they
should look up Osbourn or Dr. Dorgan if they ever
wanted a side hustle. It seems they were also
selectively outsourcing to particularly "skilled"
hypnotists with "flexible" views on ethics.

My mind shot back to the "advanced hypnokink"
events, could Osbourn have been using these events to
funnel "field hands" in? To assess their "skills"
and character (or lack there of) before making them
an offer??

I'd never heard of this Mr. Dordon character before.

So, of course , as soon as my interaction with the
death row inmate was over- that's exactly who I
researched.

A simple google search, thru a VPN on a burner device
, provided me with a new and truly horrifying suite
of information.

Apparently, he was a clinical Psychotherapist and
certified hypnotist who- instead of utilizing his

education for helping humanity in literally ANY way-
had turned his skills into a weapon for satisfying
his own lusts for power and control and providing
online confirmation bias for individuals who shared
his more concerning apparent slants.

Perhaps even (somehow) worse? It seems he, with help
from his partner, was literally attempting to
normalize not only hypnosis for sexual power but
also- and I quote- playing with "death fantasies".

Yes, you (sadly) read that correctly.

They had performed at a spinoff of the large kink
convention in the peninsula , that was hosted in the
northwest. But where they really shined was on their
own webpage, where they encouraged people with a DEATH
FANTASY to "explore" it with the help of hypnosis.

There was also- obviously - a slant towards
dollification/ other de-personalization hypnosis
niches and an overall very master/ owner -slave/
possession vibe about it all. There was blatant
mention of ties to the very same cult that Osbourn
had professed to be a member of. Specifically, his
partner openly identified as a blood fetishist and a
follower of Dhelma.

You know, I feel like "death fantasy" and "blood
fetishism" had another name before it had a label
slapped on it and the wonder of confirmation bias
via the internet:

"homicidal tendencies" perhaps?

Does labeling something really make it more
acceptable or any less unhinged??

I get exploring the self , but frankly the fear of
public- of scene- ridicule, of being accused of "kink

shaming", seems to be facilitating something much worse: normalizing legitimately dangerous and frankly deranged behavior and mind sets.

I wholeheartedly believe there can be and is a such thing as healthy and truly consensual kink, but labeling something as "kink" doesn't make it so. And we can say "but where's the line then?" and make it complicated, but is it really?

How about: "do no (actual) harm." If someone's "kink" or fantasies revolve around doing actual harm- if it involves death, drawing blood, amputation, murder etc- or crossing the line of true consent, then a therapist is a better call than a scene partner.

No one can help what they want naturally, what they're drawn to- but we can help, and we are responsible for what we do with it.

Much like finding someone who's suicidal doesn't justify murdering them, finding someone who's "willing" to "allow" you to actually harm them in no way takes away the ethical liability for doing so. And to think I thought it couldn't possibly get anymore disconcerting, fantastic.

Oh, and guess where this hypno death man and bride of Chuckie were leading events next? Why Osbourn's space, of course.

Unforeseen Circumstances

Like I mentioned, I had managed to do reverse image searches on some of the attendees at the hypnokink hangout I crashed, and had identified the ones of note. I had a running list on each along with all the info on their online and physical presence I could find. I also had a much longer list with the same information on my new dark web "friends" from the servers I'd managed to get accesses to with my part acting, part deep fake videos.

I'd identified scores of victims and found the ones that were still living, as it looked like there was an undeniable link between a portion of these victims and suicide, as well as more than a few "disappearances".

I had cross referenced the MaSU members I could find on the BDSM dating and hookup site with the acquaintances of Osbourn and Gandolf man and I had a growing list of known and suspected members of O.D.O. who were viable prospects for I.C.O.M.

I'd even joined a few NLP and hypnosis meet up groups and got some additional names thru their membership list to cross reference in the ever-growing sinister Venn diagram that was emerging.

I was, in many ways, at the height of my investigation, but after Gandolf man - and finally cutting off Spyder for good - I knew I had to be careful; they knew too much . Whether they were directly involved or not, there was a good chance that someone in their circle could be.

I needed to take some time off any investigating- even digitally. I had to be careful about risking too much further contact, too many more questions online, or these guys would get spooked or worse, figure out who I was... if they hadn't already.

I was already terrified of what I'd stumbled on, and that's when I heard the news.

I was listening to a daily true crime news podcast when I heard the update on a certain prisoner, who had claimed to be part of I.C.O.M. It seems that despite his already being scheduled to die, someone got a bit antsy.

Well, that's not how the news spun it, of course. In true Epstein fashion, he was found dead in his cell by "suicide". Perhaps the max facility would convince a majority this was indeed the case, but I knew in the pit of my stomach that there were some powers that even bars couldn't keep you safe from.

In both Epstein's case and this unfortunate bastard's, I can't say the world will miss them- but the secrets they took to their grave ? The other soulless monsters their perishing shielded?

That's the true tragedy. Also, this revelation undoubtedly suggested the perhaps obvious, that the last shred of my idealism was hoping against: there had to be -at very least- some guard or prison staff involvement. How many positions of power had their members infiltrated??

Was nothing safe ?

Was nothing sacred??

I was in <u>WAYYY</u> over my head.

What if they knew? What if they'd found out about our letters, our emails?

If they could get to him in prison, who's to say they couldn't get to me?

Just how many powerful players were wrapped up in this shit? Who could I trust?

I was contemplating what to do , both in furthering my growingly more risky investigating and also what to do with what I'd already uncovered.

To be honest, it was just SO MUCH;

it was just SO bad.

I found myself suffering with a blanket of near debilitating heaviness. It got to the point where the bouts of catatonic made even mobilizing basic daily functions challenging at times.

I wasn't giving up, not by a long shot, but I was exhausted.

I just needed a second to breathe, a second to pretend anything was "normal" or "ok".

That's when I met HIM.

The Detective

I'd given up, assumed I was meant to be alone... that maybe it was better that way.

I think it had to be him or it wouldn't have been anyone.

I mean, who else would really get my crazy ass life, this deranged quest- who else but him??

We met in a coffee shop, on Halloween- naturally.

I was dressed as Cat Woman, because, childhood hero's.

Though, I suppose she was actually more of a villain? Then again, I'm not sure. Didn't she always seem like a bit of an anti-hero, or an "anti-villain"?

She wasn't harmless, perhaps had questionable motives but still retained some sense of ethics- even if somewhat unorthodox ones. She played by her own rules, but she did have rules. I mean in contrast to someone like the joker character, she looked like a fucking saint. Still, she could never really be fully trusted , because at the end of the day- if push came to gunfight- she really only looked out for herself and her pets.

Why her pets? I guess she just enjoyed their company, and they were a bit of an extension of herself- to allow someone to fuck with her cats was to allow someone to disrespect her by extension, one could say.

You can't fully trust an anti-hero or an anti-villain perhaps, but you can infallibly trust their nature . And I'd venture to say, you can't truly trust any human , only their nature.

At least the "anti- 's" natures tend to be a bit more reliable.

Where is that magical line between hero and anti-hero? I don't know, maybe anti-heroes do things hero's won't, can't.

What's the line between anti-villain and villain?

Who the fuck knows...

But perhaps we all feel it , to some extent- even if semantics get in the way... even if we can't fully express it, articulate it, in words .

Most little kids grow up wanting, being taught by society to want,

to need-

to search for- a hero.

A hero, we're told, is someone who feels safe and acts kind and good and will save us from the monsters that plague us.

Most adults, I'm convinced , still desperately yearn for the same, someone- anyone- to protect them , someone to rely on, someone stable, someone they can trust...

someone to rescue them.

He was not in costume, but looked like he was plotting something himself. He sat at a corner table, that was partially obscured by a mess of fake spiderwebs , hunched over an open laptop and a surprisingly fru fru lavender frozen latte. The bright purple beverage, adorned with an oversized gummy spider added a note of endearing discrepancy to his otherwise rigid demeanor and large, lanky frame.

He wasn't physically my type- more like the antithesis of it, with his blindingly pale skin stretched almost skeletally over a 6 ft 3 frame. He looked to be in his mid 30's despite his weathered expression and balding head.

I wasn't attracted to him sexually, but I was strangely drawn- curious you could say- and nothing bad ever comes from that, right?

So, I struck up a conversation, asked what he was working on. He smiled a peculiar, almost boyish grin, looked over his shoulder and answered simply, "I'm an investigator of sorts".

Naturally, though skeptical, I was also hopelessly intrigued.

I didn't know until we got to know each other much more intimately, and far after we'd become "intimate" , that he was a homicide detective with the Sherriff's department .

I'd thought he was a private eye at first, mostly because he strongly led me to believe so, and dodged any of my more probing questions, for (literally) months.

I was a bit unsure how I felt about this revelation at first, but I earnestly wanted to believe it was possible for there to be people in the law enforcement industry for the right reasons.

I mean who doesn't grow up secretly wanting a real
life "hero" to swoop in and save them from their
monsters ... from their own tendency to get mixed up
with them?

I was a cynic- sure- and fiercely independent; I
always have been. But with independence, with time,
comes a deep gnawing sense of obliterating
exhaustion. I just wanted to feel safe for a minute,
to be able to fucking breathe for a second - to let
someone else take watch so I could get some damn
rest, just for a moment.

After giving up the "dangerous" bad boy (the sadist)
I'd accidentally fallen for, I suppose this new ,
clean cut, boyish man seemed like the "safe" , "sane"
choice... and boy had my life been devoid of both
concepts as of late.

So, I took a chance, rolled those dice; I let him in.

And more rapidly than made (any) logical sense, I
started to fall for this "hero".

Of course I'd fall hopelessly in love with my real
life version of the old English detective character
I'd swooned over for most of my life, but it was so
much more than that.

I'd sworn I was done trying in the "love" department,
but this guy was literally related to the great
hunting cap detective from my childhood novels (or
so he said).

I was taken back by how quickly I was willing to
give up this crazy quest I'd found myself on, just
to keep him safe ... just to be with him.

I thought for a second that maybe, just maybe, I
COULD have it. You know, that allusive "it" that

everyone else seemed to eventually find: love,
security ... or at very least something stable and
normal and not life threatening or heart wrenching.

He seemed nothing like any man I'd ever been with, or
ever known- right down to his crystal, piercing,
blue eyes.

"Different" - as may be obvious at this point- seemed
like a VERY good thing.

He brought me a single yellow rose on our second
date, he made dinner reservations, opened car doors,
listened when I talked, held my hair back when I was
sick and came to my rescue when my car battery died.

The car assistance was offered in such an endearing
manner that, despite my fiercely independent nature, I
not only let him assist me but also couldn't wipe
the idiotic grin off my face all day.

I guess somewhere between the weekends spent wandering
China town and the tapas nights spent with a platter
of goodness atop his bed with our latest bingeworthy
sitcom,

somewhere at the intersection of deep chats late into
the night and our escalating sexual exploration-

it got serious.

Grant it, he certainly helped this along via
constantly pushing the envelope sexually and
emotionally .

Before I knew it, I was hand dyeing him tie-dye,
writing him disgustingly romantic notes and hiding
them in his car, reading him my poetry, letting him
see me cry. I even painted him a fucking portrait of

our hands holding each other... a picture which made
me sigh a lot, despite the unmistakable and growing
urge to strike myself.

I guess what I'm saying is, I fell into a temporary
state of manic delusion- of stupidly gregarious ,
giddy insanity.

I fell into, well, "love" - though I hadn't allowed
myself to say it yet.

I always said I hoped to feel real love from a man
before I died- but once I felt I did , I found that I
didn't want to die at all... until we were sexy old
people and we fell asleep forever in each other's
arms... possibly in a rose garden by the water,
probably after a lot of good wine and lots of kinky
sex -

not that I'd thought about it or anything.

I actually felt (almost) safe when we were together.
Nothing-

NOTHING-

was worth risking that,

not even continuing digging, using myself as bait,
engaging with those monsters.

So, reluctantly, once he'd asked me to be his
girlfriend (officially) I backed off digging. I
stopped going to events.

He asked me incredibly early on to be "exclusive" -
like within a week of meeting. I was hesitant and
originally put him off. However, after a month of
him swooping in to be my listening ear, taking me on
proper dinner dates, bringing me flowers and bearing

what seemed like an intact soul, I caved and agreed
to be "exclusive" .

I didn't tell him about my "project" right away, but
I also couldn't really ethically justify continuing
to go on playdates with my targets or using (mostly)
fake videos of myself as bait while I was in an
actual exclusive relationship. So I told myself I'd
just press pause, I needed time to think and decide
my next route of attack anyway. Still, I'd gotten
so used to digging , so used to my alter ego - it'd
become a bit hard to tell where she ended and I began.
The line had grown dotted, like those ones on the
street - the white ones that signal it's ok to pass
or merge as you please, as long as you're going in
the same general direction. The line was also faded
with all the crossing over , and honestly, I was
finding it a bit hard to give up "Ember" completely.

Wildfire

It was moving fast with this detective man, but despite some naturally occurring (for me) feelings of panic, I was mostly ok with it.

Within a few months of dating, he was talking about getting a place together. I told him I was open to the future possibility, but that it was just wayyy too early to talk cohabitation.

Still, we were pretty damn near cohabitation, spending almost every night together- save the occasional call out, where he'd receive a call and have to leave in the middle of the night to deal with work stuff. I always felt so bad for him, having to leave and go into the cold, dark night with no notice - to deal with murder.

I was surprised he still drank on his "call out" nights, but he didn't seem drunk, and I figured it wasn't really my place to judge.

He also told me he loved me during this time period, and I surprised myself by not only believing it, but also reciprocating it.

He'd sometimes jokingly bring it up after, like if we were having a debate about something dumb- like say the merits of celery or what bagel was the best kind - he'd look at me with that devious smile and those still, crystal eyes and ask, "Do you love me?"

"Yes, of course" I'd respond with a smile and an eye roll. Usually this sickeningly cute exchange would be followed up with kisses and embrace, but sometimes - well one time- it was followed up with another question.

"Would you kill for me?" he asked, a different kind of look filling his eyes. I wasn't sure what the look was, almost manic? Yet that same comfortingly familiar devious grin was there to let me know he was joking...

"I mean, he must be joking-", I reasoned.

"If anyone hurts you? I think I'd have to..." I answered with a laugh and followed it up with, "- really though, that's awful -" laughing again.

For an instant, his eyes shot an almost annoyed glance, but quickly softened to laughter also.

He had such a dark sense of humor sometimes, but who could fucking blame him with what he'd seen...

 with what he'd seen.

and I didn't know the half of it.

Spill

After several months of dating, and reluctantly distancing myself from further investigation... after he told me he loved me, I figured it was high time I let him into the fullness my fucked up little world.

So, one rainy Saturday afternoon, we sat down, and I finally told him everything. He took it surprisingly well but was understandably concerned for our safety. I thought with his profession, perhaps he'd have the connections and know how to assist me in what to do with all the dirt I'd found, ideally without coming to an untimely demise myself.

When he didn't seem interested in getting involved, I was a bit taken back, but decided not to push it for the time being. I figured he was probably just in shock; it was admittedly a lot to take in.

I reasoned that, in time, he'd open up to the idea of helping me in my strange quest, or at very least be a good resource if I needed police level access. He had made it clear early on that he had no issue with grey area utilization of his resources. I guess normal people would see this as a really bad sign, but I suppose I saw it as useful at the time.

Frankly, I also saw it as kinda hot because- as he'd never shown me reason to think he used it for anything extreme or bad- I figured fuck yeah, use what you've got as long as it's for the greater good... as long as you're just weaving over the dotted white line. And, to clarify, the "grey area" that he spoke of consisted of things like tormenting DV abusers via text or stalking back stalkers.

I'd "joked" how I really hoped he was as great as he seemed, as I'd be royally fucked if he wasn't.

He laughed. "What do you mean?" he asked with a devious smile.

"I don't know, you're twice my size, a techy, well connected , armed and a fucking cop-" I offered with a laugh and an eye roll.

"- and I know how to make murder look like suicide," he offered, apparently continuing my dark humor masking actual concern.

"What? That's fucking awful, stop." I laughed.

Our macabre line of conversation, ended with him offering additional reassurance that he was not like everyone else, that he'd never do what they had to me... that I was finally really, truly "safe".

I was happy that when I'd opened up to him about Ember, I found that I wasn't the only one with kinks. He never would really go into detail about what his entailed (I assumed he was shy, although he didn't seem demure in any other area of life), but he did maintain that he was into the idea also. He seemed to mostly just like the idea of kink, the "taboo" of it all, I guess.

So, we played with that a bit. It started small, as he didn't really seem very experienced and seemed oddly almost threatened that I was. But then it grew, and before I knew it, he wanted more and more.

Within 6 months or so, even the most objectively edge play related experimentation seemed to grow boring for him - at an alarmingly rapid rate. I did know he was a bit of a thrill junkie going in, but I

guess it was just surprising since he had always
maintained that sex was an "emotional connection"
thing for him. I remember, because he seemed visibly
aggravated when I shared that it had never been
emotional *for* me, and I didn't know if it ever would
be.

I thought maybe he was trying to prove himself in
some misguided and completely unnecessary way, but
then again, it never seemed like it was about me, at
all.

If we were in public, he wasn't interested in
watching me, he was interested in using me to provoke
reactions from onlookers... he was watching them,
their reactions;

It was never about me.

I talked to him about it, but I mostly just
dismissed it, figuring, he was probably just green
to it all and finding his way... maybe insecure and
overcompensating or something.

To be fair, he'd had a hell of a couple of years,
that would make anybody a bit "off".

Which, I guess, is the same reasoning I used to
dismiss his growingly frequent outbursts and
sometimes callous disregard at things that hurt me.

Mommy Dearest

He had mentioned pretty early on that his mother had passed away within the last year or two, that was the reason he was living with his dad, back in his old childhood attic bedroom.

He had told me that she had been an alcoholic and that their relationship was strained and complicated by the end.

He told me through, well not exactly tears, but through quite audible sobs that his mom had gone out at her own hand.

My empathy was immediately hemorrhaged. To see such a big guy, with an oddly boyish quality to him, cry like that ... it moves you; it moves anybody.

I noticed the lack of tears thing, but then he volunteered that he had chronically dry eyes- which explained all the eye drop containers I'd found around the house and in his car.

Still, moisture or not, it was heart wrenching. He told me that he was the first on the scene. He'd even handled processing the body with his department. I felt a stab of emotion at the latter and started tearing up myself. How strong do you have to be to process the scene, the body , of your own mother ???

It was unthinkable.

He mentioned in passing something about how there were other things , at the scene ... that he changed it , that he felt he had to- to "spare the family more pain".

He didn't go into detail, I don't think he even ever said what method she used to take her own life, but I wasn't gonna quiz him on something so painful and so recent in the grand scope of things.

I was just so blown away at how he was still going . Not only had he endured the tragic loss of his mother , he explained, he had also been in a volatile relationship with a woman who he said very much reminded him of his mom. He said that relationship ended just after his mother's ashes were scattered.

These dates would fluctuate and the timelines he shared were both vague and seemed to keep morphing, but again, who the fuck could really blame him for being hazy on temporal details when faced with so much grief at once.

He painted the ex as violent- though the only example he'd provided was her own apparent suicide attempt when they were together. He said she had told people he had abused her ... that she was out to get him fired and that she was making things up.

I thought this last one must have been extra painful, as he'd already told me how his mother had accused him of the same - even though he told me, she was the one who'd grown violent towards the end.

He said that his mother had also been threatening to get him fired too, before her untimely and tragic end.

It sounded like his ex was really callous to the loss of his mother, she didn't even come with him to scatter the ashes (of his cremated mom); he never said why. I guess they broke up soon after. In fact, he said she moved out of the state entirely and dropped all contact after the split. I suppose that explained why there didn't seem to be anything current when I'd tried googling her name, that or perhaps she just kept a low profile like myself.

His mom though, I guess she must have had a change of heart at the end, because he did mention that she had been clasping a picture of him when she died ... I didn't really get why that would be something he'd need to alter or hide or how it would hurt his family more, but again , I was there to listen, not demand answers or details from my grieving partner.

Despite all the pain he shared, all the sorrows he'd fallen victim to, his reactions to my own tidbits of the mountain of trauma I'd been through, were met with less than ideal responses. "It's hard to be with a victim"... a phrase he actually uttered more than once in response to my shares. Besides being incredibly callous and hurtful, it was pretty laughably hypocritical.

I reasoned, however, it was likely the result of his own inability to process his experiences and more of a self-blaming reaction than anything directly aimed at or about me. So, reluctantly, I decided to shrug it off for the time being, in hopes with time and support he would process things enough to be less of an asshole. Basically? I (again) allowed my empathy to blind me to the seeming complete lack of the same quality in my partner.

Into The Flames

Our relationship went to a really intense and really serious level -in all the ways- really fast. I mostly chalked this up to us both being exceedingly blunt and intense people who didn't like to play games or waste time, as well as a lot of outside contributing factors that intensified our sense of urgency- like his insane day to day at work and my, well, just life really... just my whole crazy, fucking life.

He was definitely the one pushing it forward, but despite a few panic attacks along the way, (I figured #trauma) I wasn't really hating it or fighting it.

It felt good to be with someone who seemed to have their shit together and who knew what they wanted.

By 4 months, I was full blown in "love", and also unemployed. I had gotten laid off for the first time in my life and it was a very disorienting time to say the least.

Right about the week after everything peaked in relational bliss- just before his journey overseas - a host of less charming, odd little qualities started emerging in "my love".

Among these less charming things I noticed about my crime fighting partner was his stubborn insistence on calling me by the same nick name my abusive ex had. I didn't blame him for using it to begin with, but after telling him (multiple) times both my preferred nick name as well as why I silently despised the one he'd been using- I DID.

He just kind of ignored me and continued using the old one, leaving me both fuming and hurt as to why he kept "forgetting" every single time. I mean I don't know which was worse, that he used the old name I hated all the time or the one time he "accidentally" called me by his ex's .

To be fair, I was shocked I hadn't been the one to call him the wrong name- it was half the reason I'd been so intentional about saying his name so much when we spoke in the beginning. Then again, I also wasn't talking about my ex all the time- and holy heck had he given me an ongoing incessant earful about his.

Good gosh , I mean, we're cooking and it's : "Ashley put dill in my pot pie once when we were cooking , it was inedible- she knew I hated dill".

We're on a romantic getaway with a jacuzzi and it's : " Ashley got naked in a hot tub once. She was clearly just trying to show off to my friend and piss me off".

Sometimes, it was just literally out of nowhere - like we're driving into Oregon and he literally just says her name like he has fucking Tourette's or something.

Side note: I'm sorry, not sorry, but if you're still pissed about a dill rich pot pie, you've lived a pretty privileged and sheltered dating experience- I didn't go on about the searing sexual abuse I'd experienced in my past relationships half as much as this guy talked about his damn pot pie.

Like I mentioned, he had said she reminded him of his mom, who he also talked about constantly. The latter I reasoned away as completely fair as she had passed

away a couple years before suddenly and tragically
and their relationship had been "complicated".

The former-the ex thing- though irritating, and sort
of confounding at times, I also excused. I
psychoanalyzed his lingering fixation to probably be
tied to her reminding him of his mom, especially with
their having broken up so shortly after her passing.

Maybe it wasn't Ashley but exes in general he was
fixated on , because he also seemed far more
interested in my exes' lives than I ever was.

I'd shared enough to justify outrage at the slew of
assholes I'd encountered, that would make sense. The
odd thing was that he seemed primarily fixated on my
ex husband- and this fixation didn't seem to start
until I expressed that I didn't know if he'd ever be
caught because he was careful and very good at the
bad things he did and covering them up.

At the last bit, he seemed jealous... like jealous at
the idea that my ex was clever even in a devious
horrid way. And that's when he suddenly seemed
fixated on my ex husband, his life and dreaming up
his destruction -to an alarming level, even for me .

It was weird when he found my ex's social media
accounts and went on about how gross he was. It was
uncomfortable when he mentioned where he lived and
that he'd looked it up (but wouldn't share it), but
it was downright inappropriate when he felt the need
to inform me that he'd found out my ex was getting
remarried.

I was confused as to why he was sharing, and also
why the fuck he cared if I didn't.

"OK?" I offered . I tried to explain that- though I
did hope he got caught- I was just happy to be free
and that I'd moved on.

This didn't stop him from sharing a disturbing
hypothetical, one Sunday afternoon a few weeks later.

How To Get Away With (Hypothetical?) Murder

We were on a beach- of the clothing optional variety.
We had developed an odd little Sunday afternoon
ritual of picnicking naked on the beach and drinking
canned Maui Tia's before getting either matcha soft
serve or shrimp filled Chinese doughnuts covered in
spicy mayo (sounds odd yes, but it's fucking
delicious).

We were setting up and cracking open that first can,
when he made some joke about my ex. I laughed, then he
continued on to a presumably related topic in his
mind , of how to get away with murder.

He said he'd thought it through- how to do it- which
was pretty noticeably apparent given the level of
detail he went into in this disturbing little macabre
monologue.

I won't detail all the nooks and crannies here, but
it involved a 3D printed weapon, using the cartridge
of one weapon and the rest of another, a burner cell
and a motorcycle (he owned 2) transported in the back
of a truck (such as the one he regularly borrowed
from his dad).

I just kind of sat in awkward silence, waiting for
him to laugh or really any sign that this was a
fucked up joke. When he finally stopped speaking, I
was met-instead- with a placid, emotionless face and
those blinking crystal blue eyes staring back at me.

"Good to know?" I offered , before continuing; "-
look, just to reiterate, I want my ex to be caught

and exposed for what he is... not... you know,
murdered. I don't want that -"

"Of course, I'm just talking -" he countered with the
laugh I'd been hoping for.

It was probably just his rage talking, because of
how much my ex had hurt me, I figured . Still, holy
fuck had he thought out murder to the last detail. I
mean it was sort of his job though, I guess,
thinking like a murderer.

But then he added one more line that kept the uneasy
bubbling up in me, "-I'm just saying , if you ever
hear that he was murdered mysteriously , it wasn't
me... just remember that it wasn't me."

I repeated my earlier sentiment about, you know, not
wanting him to murder anyone- but he just said
again, "I'm just saying, it won't be me-".

My detective never really brought up my ex much after
that day- which was odd but a welcome change.

My ex-husband was a monster, and if he did die, there
would be no tears on my end. Still, justice-
vengeance- was exposure not bloodlust, and frankly I
didn't want him to go out that easy. And as, unlike
Fuckface, my ex-husband hadn't inserted himself into
my new life, I didn't see any logical reason for
extreme measures.

Was this "hypothetical" murder plot gallows' humor ?
I sure hoped so.

Not that I hadn't thought about it. Fuck, sometimes
I even felt guilty for not wiping him out when I
could have. Maybe I wasn't strong enough too, or
maybe I just couldn't help picturing how hard his
mother would have cried if I had. She didn't deserve

to lose a son, even if he was (likely unbeknownst to her) a monster.

But then again, the women and children he hurt , has hurt, will hurt...

Is hurting ...

scarring,

maybe worse,

they don't deserve that either.

If removing one life saves another, is that justice... is that just?

To some extent our "justice" system is based on this idea: protecting society from those monsters that just won't stop hurting.

Where's the line??

Was I responsible for those he hurt after me, because my inaction allowed him-in essence- to keep hurting ?

Not legally, maybe not even ethically, but there was an aspect of responsibility- of something- that I just couldn't shake.

If I'd had "proof", maybe I could have done it "the justice system" way. Unfortunately, like many of the worst monsters, he was careful- and I had nothing but the unbearably crushing, uncomfortably clear circumstantial evidence, combined with my own scarring experience .

Some would say Karma's a bitch and the justice system grinds slowly but it grinds.

But what about everyone who's annihilated in the meantime ?

And what about the predators that slip through the cracks without ever getting caught?

What's OUR responsibility? As individuals , as a society ... as humans?

Perhaps Granny would mention how the Bible says "-vengeance is mine, says the Lord." Or "The Bible says to love your neighbor."

I'd argue however, that yes, maybe the pedophile across the street is technically my neighbor, but so are the flocks of children he scars with his selfish, evil predation. If I really love those kids and their families- my neighbors- how can I not do something about it?

But what is there really to be done?

Still, if anyone really claims to follow this teaching- this sentiment- how can we "allow" a single individual to continue to plague dozens of lives with their evil choices? How can we not act to stop it if given any actual opportunity ... no matter the cost to us personally?

Maybe blind rebel justice does equal anarchy and chaos, but turning a blind eye ... ignoring suffering because it's not "your business" ... when good people do nothing ?

It may just be worse.

Is "justice " my job... is it yours?

I tend to think it's all of ours.

Along Granny's similar reasoning, yes- praying is important, necessary- but what about "being his hands and feet"?

What about action?

I'm not saying murder, but action.

What about our responsibilities?

Where's the line??

I don't know the answer to the question, I'm just posing it.

I will say, maybe if you're praying for a hole and God gives you a shovel,

well maybe you should just start digging.

And I pray-

I do, not for him ...

No.

I pray for everyone in his path- that he never hurts anyone again, that he's made incapable of doing so ever again, whether it be via "salvation" or by some kind of demise.

As I thought of how much horror and heartache- how much destruction- that one man can bring, it made me consider: don't I have the same power, the same obligation- almost- to bring an equal onslaught of good into the rotting universe?

Don't we all?

I didn't take him out, I wasn't willing to trade my life for his. So, I sure as fuck better make sure it was worth it... that I equal out the evil he will continue to bring.

Maybe that's one way in a broader sense, that we can all fight the destroyers: by challenging ourselves to be equally motivated but in a completely opposite direction as the vile that we encounter.

Secrets, Secrets Are No Fun; Secrets, Secrets-

There were several strange tiny closets in the upper room of his father's house, the one he said used to be a "haunted" attic when he was a child and had later been renovated into his bedroom.

I'd commented on these, the one behind the stacks of pictures above his bed, the one crammed shut behind his bed- jokingly asking if that's where he kept the bodies.

Without missing a beat, he returned, with equal parts monotone and what I assumed (hoped) to be dark humor with "Yes, that's where Sarah and Conner are".

I laughed, and asked, " Oh ? and who are they?"

He calmly informed me that Sarah was his girlfriend and Conner was his son-but they wouldn't be bothering us -in fact, they didn't talk much at all anymore.

"That's horrible " I countered with a laugh, my eyes still tracing over the mysterious little closets.

He'd bring up Sarah and Conner every now and then in passing, always with that same unaffected far off smile. It was a bit off-putting sure, but to be fair, I figured the guy probably had to have a healthy dose of gallows humor to get through a decade on the force and seeing all the things that went along with it.

He did finally show me the inside, or at very least the entry way of the inside of the two little closets, which appeared from what I could see in the

darkness to be exceedingly more expansive than I'd
previously assumed. He joked that maybe one day he'd
tie me up and keep me there for a day or two. I took
this to be a scene proposal, so I laughed and
responded with a "Maybe one day, we can talk about
it,".

I kind of put it out of my mind, but then he left
for an extended trip to Europe.

I wasn't trying to snoop, ok... I wasn't.

I just happened to see the shoebox lying there on his
lower shelf below the tiny closet. It was labeled
"yesteryear" and I guess I felt oddly drawn to take a
peek.

He was in Europe for two weeks, and had insisted I
take a key to his place and crash there. I was
feeding his cat, watering the roses and enjoying the
extra space. The shoebox was something I discovered
after a couple glasses of wine and a cigar and
watching movies got too boring. I lifted the lid
cautiously and found a stack of old pictures,
polaroids not unlike the type made by the camera he'd
just bought me, but these were definitely close to a
decade old. There was nothing crazy in them- nothing
immediately sinister really. The first picture was of
his cat as a kitten , then the rose bushes out front,
then I came across one of a woman I recognized as his
late mother. She was smiling in the picture , not at
all seeming like the monster he painted her to be. She
didn't look like much of a drunk either, but I guess
you never can tell.

Just as I was about to put the stack back- a tinge
of guilt suddenly springing up in me for looking in
his personal things while he was away - my eyes fell
on a picture of something else.

It was a picture of him as a younger man , a boy
really, maybe 17 ? It was the first picture I'd seen
of him as a teen. He was with a young girl of maybe
16 and they appeared to be dressed in formal attire -
some type of prom ? She had on an emerald colored
silk dress and held a corsage with a huge smile. She
had green eyes just like mine, and I couldn't help
but notice, blazing red hair- incredibly similar to
the color of mine...

the color he'd said he was crazy about .

I flipped over the picture and felt a slight tinge of
uneasy , as I read the inscription in one of the
yellowed corners that had been scrawled in black felt
pin: "Donny and Sarah- senior prom 2010".

My phone suddenly rang and I -startled- dropped the
box and all its' contents on the ground in my
surprise.

"Fuck!"

I picked up the phone beside me - hands still
trembling a bit, and saw an incoming call,

from Donny.

After a few rings, with my heart beating wildly as
my finger hovered over the screen, I pushed ignore.

I stooped down to pick up the contents from the
shoebox, that now neatly littered the hall, doing my
best to replace them as I found them. I straightened
the stack out and scolded myself for fucking with
things I shouldn't, before quickly placing
everything back in the box and returning it to its
home on the shelf under the tiny closet that was
behind the maritime picture over the bed.

I went into the kitchen and poured myself a drink to steady my hands before I called him back.

For a moment , I thought he sounded off with overly syrupy pleasantries perhaps cloaking something not unlike anger? After chatting for an hour, however, I convinced myself it must just be my conscience smarting me for snooping.

It was odd- the contents of the box- but, then again, if someone looked into my shit they'd find plenty to fit that descriptor too . I tried to just put it out of my head.

Whitewashed Death

Before long, Donny was back in town. I tried to just brush off the strange findings and the odd beachside murder hypotheticals, and all the existential pondering they'd brought on. I had my hands "kind of" full at the time.

I was dealing with my first layoff amid two (previously booked and naturally nonrefundable) international trips, the beginnings of an unrelated legal battle , major dental surgery, a recent (also unrelated... fuck humanity sometimes ...) active shooter situation and navigating several rather unwelcome and horrifyingly unpleasant flash-back-y realizations about some experiences in my past. The latter (probably) brought to me (at least in part) compliments of said layoff and the accompanying (mostly) unwelcome unpaid time off it afforded, mixed with the (also aforementioned) running from an active shooter experience.

Well, there was all THAT and the whole dating someone seriously, and thus fully attempting to trust for the first time after a lifetime of people showing me repeatedly that humans are mostly garbage and my trust and love is typically rewarded with scalding betrayal and life threatening violence, abuse and stalking.

You know, there was that, in addition to the naturally all encompassing, ever present anxiety that accompanies single handedly attempting to take down an underground empire of sadistic, rape-y, amateur hypnotists who are linked to a cult based secret society who like to torture subby ladies for kicks and have been engaging in an intricate network of

international sex trafficking without any detection
for like a century.

So, no big!

I was fucking fantastic.

I was in a glorious state of mind for rational
thought when it came to navigating interpersonal
relationships with zero frame of reference for
"normal" or "healthy".

So, when my "hero" suddenly started making jokes
about torture in a sexual context, making victim
blaming comments about DV survivors and gas lighting
me after his outbursts - I guess I just wasn't
really in a place to fully process it all, go
figure.

I made excuses for everything he did, for everything
he said, everything he put me through.

Even an especially odd comment he made as we fell on
the topic of mortality one evening as we sat in his
bed, watching some vampire comedy, enjoying one of
our "platter nights" as we called them (we made tapas
and ate them on platters in bed ... with a lot of
booze).

I had started talking about cemeteries- as one had
been pictured in the vampire show we were watching. I
was talking about how I enjoyed going to ancient
cemeteries because they were oddly beautiful, but that
I disliked being near newer ones as it seemed too
eerie and more often than not, flung me into an
uncomfortable existential crisis.

He went along with the musings, adding with a far
off gaze, " Yeah and there's all these people who did
awful things ... that no one ever found out. They

took their atrocities to their grave , while everyone
remembers them as a pillar of society" . I glanced
over with an inquisitive stare, but all I was met
with was an eerily serene countenance laced with a
faint (self-satisfied?) smile.

The discussion, the moment- it reminded me of a
passage from my youth... something Christ had said
about the people who his own society perhaps mistook
as "heroes". He said these hypocrites , in so many
words- these fakes- they were like white washed tombs.
They were clean and serene on the outside , but full
of only death and darkness.

I Wanna Run Away (Again)

Right before our 1 year anniversary of meeting, we had a discussion. He had pissed off more than a few dangerous people in his job and the threat on my safety was also very real-and would only escalate once I released what I'd found. So, we decided to disappear - together.

He would medically retire, and we'd use his professional knowledge and access to effectively disappear and make a fresh start, and then I'd publish. At his suggestion we migrated to a temporary safehouse together, which was basically a by the month house in the suburbs full of the whitest, richest people I'd ever seen. We moved in together a few months after his return from Europe. I wasn't thrilled about the safe house, it was beyond not my scene, but it was only going to be for a couple months while we prepared for our get away.

At first, I was thrilled about the plan, and he seemed like he was too. Maybe all we needed was a change of scenery, a fresh start, I thought.

As the proposed date of our departure approached, however, he started to seem different - or maybe the eerie silence of the burbs and cohabitation just made me notice it more. I reasoned that he was probably just stressed.

It was peculiar, it started to feel like he could read my mind those last couple of months, before "the ordeal". He would casually bring up things I'd only told my mom on the phone - once or twice I could have brushed off, but it was much more than that.

It didn't make any sense. The only way it DID make sense, was if he was somehow able to listen in on my conversations.

To be fair, I knew he could have easily bugged my phone or the whole fucking house if he had wanted to. Besides having ample access to both, he neglected to mention until 3 months into us dating, that he was a cyber security and OSINT expert at work (around the same time he cheerfully added how much he'd studied blood splatter analysis and CSI). It wasn't that he "couldn't" have, I just didn't think - I just couldn't bring myself to believe- that he would.

I decided to test it , before we ran away together. I had to know I could trust him, and that was getting harder by the day. He just seemed different, colder ... more cocky, almost angry? Yeah, that was it; he seemed like he was fuming underneath that smile that cut thru his face every time I walked into the room.

Maybe I was just being paranoid. I mean , being doxed and hunted , then hunting , then pissing off and being targeted by an underground group of sadistic hypnotists who were peripherally involved with an extremist cult will kind of do that to you . Also, there were the little things along the way that he sprinkled in. His control issues seemed to be increasing, I reasoned he was just trying to keep me "safe" . The gaslighting and angry "PTSD" outbursts-always directed at me for some reason- those were harder to explain away.

I figured that perhaps he was just nervous about the plan, maybe I was. I mean, we couldn't have asked for a more "tense" set of circumstances.

I wanted to trust him, but something was stopping me.

I have PTSD, but I never directed my reactions at
him. I never treated him like he treated me. Also, as
outlandish as it sounded, I couldn't shake the
feeling that he was watching when I wasn't looking
... listening when I wasn't aware.

So, I told myself I'd just test it. I wouldn't tell
anyone, I'd just test it before I went "all in". I
typed the words into google , while connected to the
fiberoptic internet he'd so kindly installed in our
dwelling when we moved in , " 3 weeks pregnant -signs
" . I clicked on a few of the resulting pages , and
scrolled thru enough to make it reasonably
believable. I tried a few more for good measure; "
abortion or adoption?", then "how to tell your
partner your expecting " . There, my trap was baited;
I figured if anything would force a reaction, it
would be a fake pregnancy, as he'd repeatedly said he
didn't want kids and had even scheduled a vasectomy
procedure for a few days before our departure.

Waiting, Watching

It had been a week and nothing new... other than his seemingly growing irritation at me, which made me question things. I was hoping that evening's activities would help. I had - reluctantly- agreed to a very unorthodox request he'd made. I knew he was a bit of an adrenaline junkie, and -to be fair- that's part of what drew me to him, as I have a healthy dose of adrenalin addiction myself.

I knew he had cave dived and liked to race motorcycles - pretty standard thrill junkie shit. There were also some smaller, day to day signs that seemed innocent, but perhaps in hindsight were telling.

For instance, he always ate huge chunks of the wasabi at our sushi dates "for the rush". I just laughed. Then, he started bringing up random offbeat things he wanted to try out of nowhere, like riding an actual bull in Spain ... or skiing during avalanche season in remote areas where we'd have to cross partially frozen lakes.

Then there was the time he tried to make a game out of attempting to run under the garage door before it crushed his body, just for the fuck of it.

I'm a bit of a thrill seeker (clearly), but I prefer calculated risk - you know, the age old "risk verses reward" system of decision making.

But him? I wasn't so sure if he calculated the same way ... or at all.

I couldn't help but feel like he was escalating in his tendency to seek out risk at all costs, both in his own life and in our experiences together. It started to feel like if things weren't constantly at a crazy level of escalating taboo in our sex life, he was growing almost bored.

I tried to ignore it, and just keep things at a comfortably above average kinky level, but his appetite for risk for the sake of risk was starting to feel unsustainable. Worse yet, each time I gave into something more taboo, it only fed his appetite for more. It went beyond use-y and close to just plain scary.

Still, I had no idea how far it went until he suggested an unusual location for our um ... debauchery .

I don't mean like on a beach, or in a winery or even in a dungeon - God knows we'd already done all of the above at my suggestion , this though - this was different .

I'd remarked how I "appreciated" the warehouse aesthetic, how it did something "special" for me. He'd first suggested we could find a warehouse, which I was all for. I figured we would "break into" an abandoned one, maybe by the water or something , as there were numerous in our general area. Even though it'd be exciting, it was also innocuous as no one really gave a shit if you fucked around in these abandoned buildings as long as you were quiet about it and didn't get yourself hurt or damage the space.

I soon learned, however, this was not what he had in mind- probably because it was pretty low risk.

No, instead , he suggested a building at his work, as in at the Sheriff's department.

"No" , was obviously my first response.

"That's way too risky! You could get fired; we could probably be arrested. Why not just go to an abandoned warehouse ??" I reasoned, but he was resolute in his insistence.

He said there was an evidence locker - which was basically a medium sized cement room with no windows that had a locked cage for evidence in the middle, he said there were no cameras and it's where they processed evidence they collected.

He claimed he could get the keys whenever he wanted, that no one would question it if he did it right.

"But why??" I reasoned again, "Why risk it??"

He insisted he wanted to be able to think about something exciting we'd done while he was at work to make his job more bearable for the last few weeks. He'd been seeming on his last leg with the job as of late, and God knows I'd been nothing but supportive in my attempts to help. This was another level ask though.

He kept up the insistence however, despite my protest - and actually started scouting out the spot and doing recon.

He'd update me daily, including that he'd "casually" double checked with a buddy that there were no cameras.

Before I knew it, after several weeks of talking about it, he'd planned what day we were to enact this deranged fantasy. I gave in, as it seemed to be happening regardless. I figured maybe it was his last fuck off to his industry before we ran away together, as was (I suppose) his growing tendency to arrive home with a beer in hand while driving his work car.

The Incident

Ok, let's talk about it... that day , the day of his
suggested workplace debauchery... the day that
changed EVERYTHING.

The whole big move thing- the disappearing act- it
really snuck up on us. Before we knew it, our
departure date was only a couple of weeks away. The
whole scene idea of his , it ended up morphing to
something much more kidnap-y than I'd imagined,
complete with him handcuffing me and putting a bag
over my head before forcing me into his work car with
darkly tinted windows and sneaking me into the locked
compound. He even made some dark joke when we were
talking about the sequence of events asking, "How do
you feel about torture". I laughed, "That's not
funny, obviously no torture - you're so dark
sometimes -" I countered with an eye roll, praying he
was strictly joking.

Then that fateful day, after work, he signed out the
keys, and packed chains and sheets and plastic with
him .

He'd planned it down to when the shifts changed, to
be sure no one would be around.

That night, once he had me handcuffed and the bag was
on my head per his script, he drove me down to the
Sheriff's department. He seemed to really be getting
into "character" - though it was a much more
sinister character than I'd imagined. He seemed to be
enjoying it, not just the "scene", but also the
obvious growing discomfort it was producing in me.

I pushed down the queasy, and reminded myself it was all just pretend; it was only pretend.

Once we were inside of the first fenced lot, still in his cop car with the darkly tinted windows, he backed into the evidence storage locker area (another fenced in area within a fenced in area). He made sure the back of his car - where I was - would not be seen by the camera outside. Once I was inside, it looked exactly as he'd described. He had given me a safe word, and I did love him. Still, I couldn't help the seemingly out of place fear that seemed to be welling up inside of me.

Despite my discomfort, I tried to go with it, as I felt an incredible amount of pressure to do so... to not "fuck it up", to make him happy . I'd already seen what happened if I communicated any feelings of discomfort or hurt suffered at his hand. It only enraged him , and led to hours of verbal abuse due to my "making him feel bad".

At least I was wrong about the surveillance - he hadn't said anything about the searches on my fake pregnancy, despite my additions of pretending to have an upset stomach the last week.

He forced me onto a chair, taped me to it and then lifted the hood off my face just enough to duct taped my mouth shut. After a few moments in complete silence and darkness, I sensed a dim light come on. He then removed the hood from my head completely, I presume so that he could watch me watch what he did next.

He started laying out plastic in front of the cage where I saw chains hanging from. I reasoned it was just so we would have less cleanup ... and perhaps it was.

But what happened next, took me by surprise.

He leaned in and looked at me. It was a different
look . In fact, he didn't much look like himself at
all. As he stared silently into my eyes, I felt
suddenly far more naked than I had on any of our
Sunday beach trips.

After a few moments of icy discomfort, he leaned in
further and bit my shoulder so hard that I let out a
muffled yelp. I winced, still shook by his force,
before he whispered into my ear slowly; "Why
Passiflora ... Why'd you look at my stuff ?"

I instinctively shook my head, terror filling my eyes
and flooding my core.

"I know ..." he whispered again, "I've been watching
... and I know about your secret ... " he stepped
back and got louder , angrier now.

"You're- JUST- LIKE - HER!" He screamed, before
punching me in the stomach and temporarily rendering
me speechless as I attempted to catch my breath and
recover from the blow.

I shot a questioning glance up at him, perhaps still
hoping against hope that this was some offbeat part
of his scene- but realizing quickly as he continued,
that it definitely was not.

"Guess you'll have to join Sarah now. I told you I
don't want kids... and I meant it. You lying BITCH!
He exclaimed, as he slapped me across the face so
hard that the chair nearly toppled over. You said
you were taking care , that it couldn't happen. You
are JUST like her.

You know, we were supposed to run away together -"
he screamed , as he pulled out several large knives

from his backpack, along with a hammer and rope and scissors .

I started shaking my head in a non-verbal but desperate "No... no.." He continued, "I was getting a vasectomy for fuck's sake, they would have had an even harder time tying me to any of them."

I couldn't breathe, due to the combination of impact and panic, which was rapidly making me feel like I may lose consciousness at any moment.

"We could have been safe-

together" he added, whispering into my ear and groping the side of my chest.

 I felt sick; this couldn't be actually happening.

I shook my head, and contemplating mentioning the searches were a farce, that I was very , very not pregnant ... but that seemed like somewhat extraneous information at this point- and I was gagged anyway.

 He continued on,

"- we were supposed to run away together, I told you sooner or later I'd need to get out of the country, but you were too stupid and distracted to ask why ... to wonder why," he continued , unwinding the rope and setting up what appeared- to my horror- to be some type of torture tray. "Now , NOW , you're gonna see first hand why ... and it'll be the last thing you ever see. I was probably going to kill you anyway - it's just too tempting , too easy. You're already disappearing , and no one will be the wiser. If your body is found- which is doubtful- I'll pin it on one of the 100 men who want you fucking dead.

I couldn't have asked for a better victim."

I was getting sicker. Sadly, he wasn't wrong on the latter bit, and yeah, no shit Columbo, it's "obvious" now-sure- now that I'm duct taped to a metal chair in an icy evidence locker with a psychopathic killer spouting a super villain script to an audience of one.

But, you know, for some reason - previous to this little weekend adventure- my boyfriend being a fucking serial killer wasn't really in the top assumptions I was making about the motivation behind his stated dreams of eventual international living.

I was starting to sweat profusely despite how frigid it was in the glorified meat locker we were in, a fact which- despite my horror- I couldn't help noticing was making the duct tape start to loosen. I willed myself not to smile at this thought or look down at my restraints.

Thanks to a lifetime with monsters, I'd instinctually pressed my wrists apart slightly when he bound them. With a little more sweat, it was just possible , I might get out of this nightmare alive and unbutchered.

Maybe if I could get this skeletal freak to keep monologuing a bit longer- which seemed like it would be more than doable seeing his intolerable tendency towards grandiose word vomit at nauseam-

yes, if he kept going on (and on), then I'd still have a chance ...

I'd still have a chance to get out of this gothic nightmare before he turned me into charcuterie.

"- But now, "

Fantastic, yes, he was indeed continuing -

"Now , I'll just need to bump up the plan a bit ,
and stick around here a little longer to avoid
suspicion ... to discover evidence of your
disappearance , and inform your grieving family.
I'll be the hero haha-" he added the latter bit with
an eerie little chuckle.

"No" - I thought so loud it was almost audible, "-
you'll PLAY the hero,".

He continued,

"Don't worry, I'll make sure I take care of the
family in a more direct way, unlike yours, their
bodies will be found. A tragic and mysterious
shooting, with an untraceable gun. You remember that,
don't you sweetie? -

Yes, the perfect crime.

I told you I knew how to get away with murder."

I instinctively lurched at him, but the tape held me
to the chair. At the mention of my family, I knew I
had to get out ... not just get out... I had to make
sure he'd never hurt anyone EVER again.

He had the gun tucked in the back of his pants, I
knew he did. But it seemed like he had his heart - or
the hole where his heart should be - stuck on a
torture, and probably rape, likely followed by a
slow and excruciating murder by 1,000 cuts style
execution ... which was good.

Ok, I mean, not "good" exactly,

but it was useful. I'd have time.

If I could get the gun before he felt like he had to
use it,

I'd have a chance.

I looked up to the corner of the room, and he saw me as I noticed a blinking light,

"Oh yeah, there is one camera ... but don't worry- it's just for my personal collection -"

I winced.

"- Oh you hadn't figured that out yet ? Yeah sweetie, I have a whole collection. You didn't think I was speaking literally when I told you Saraha was in my closet did you ? The stench would have given me away immediately. No, I made sure her body would never be found - dropped it down a mind shaft in Nevada-

but my trophy stash?

Saraha's last moments as well as the others? They made it into my little treasure trove."

-"Sweetie" I couldn't help that this new term of endearment for me, one I'd mistakenly thought of as "tender" until today, somehow stood out even starker and more cutting in his monologue than the realization that he'd been hoarding self-directed snuff films of his victims in his tiny closet I'd slept beside for months.

Also? I couldn't help the stream of internal dialog that started in the middle of his continued villainous monologue.

"I should have known he was a psychopath... I mean what kind of monster actually considers rice crispies a 'treat' post- pubescence??!

I mean there was that and the repeated concussions from sports and fights he'd mentioned, probably resulting in frontal lobe damage.

There was his complete lack of any emotive response or facial reaction to blood or torture scenes or human suffering (other than his own, naturally, however minute).

There was his commenting how he wanted to join the bomb squad with the FBI, so that he could learn how to 'take care' of anyone who fucked with him.

Then we have his supposed childhood neglect and clear disdain for his mother and the ex who he insisted reminded him of his mother to an abnormal level,

his incessant monologuing about his mother and his ex ... his hatred of which he'd probably used, however irrationally, to 'justify' his disdain for all women and resulting 'punishment' of them (woe is you poor, persecuted incel).

There was the fact that despite all his demonstratively noisy, self-indulgent, spontaneous and usually situationally conveniently sobbing throughout our relationship - I'd never seen him actually shed a single tear.

There was the fact that all the verifiable details in his stories seemed to morph or be missing entirely,

and his mention of how he had voluntarily sat with people on their death bed without pay and how he had at nauseum told me eerily flatly about watching the life leave their eyes... and being the last one to see it.

Then there was the fact that he always volunteered to do all the autopsies for the other detectives, that time he described in detail what they did (exactly) during it... making sure to include the part about what happens to the genitalia. There was that strange far off glazed over way he said it all. I thought it was dissociation, but that wasn't quite it... was it?

He'd even insisted on being the cop present for , handling , his own mother's autopsy for fuck's sake. I mean, he said he'd been the one to 'handle' the body the whole way.

And then, oh fuck... then there was the matter of his mother.

The tragic 'suicide', that he was the 1st to the scene to... that he 'took care of', the scene he'd told me repeatedly that he'd altered, to 'protect the family from more pain'.

He'd said she was violent at the end , before ...

before threatening to get him fired.

Then there was that time a few months previous he'd told me in passing how he'd even told the guys at work if they wanted to fire him they'd have to bring a chopper and a swat team because he'd fight to the end, he wouldn't go easy.

There was that eerie comment about people taking atrocities to their grave.

Also, I don't know, there was the fact that the week when I found the old picture of Sarah, I was literally chased by a vulture for a mile and a half during my beachside run;

I mean, if that isn't an omen I don't know what is."

He started up again, as he sharpened the blade of one of the knives, shaking me from my cynical internal musings-

"Once I did the first one- or I suppose some would call it the first two- and hid her last moments in my closet... I realized how much I liked it . Then the next- well you're no detective but I'm sure you've pieced together who that was. I made sure it looked like a tragic unavoidable ending to a troubled life.

I knew after a couple of people close to home, I had to change it up to avoid suspicion, so I started going for randoms: 'the less dead': the homeless , runaways , dv victims , prostitutes - the latter are my favorite, and my job basically feeds them to me.

 Sometimes I give them a few drops, to knock them out... "

I was instantly flooded with the memory of all those eye drop containers he kept around- but he was continuing before I could finish my thought.

"-then I take them somewhere private - so I can take my time with them. They wake up groggy, scared, confused... no idea what happened- what's about to happen- to them . That's when the real fun begins-" he paused , and let out a slow exhale of delight.

He leaned in again, staring down my frame, his mouth inches from by neck , till I could feel the heat of his breath with every syllable he uttered ... till the tingling of terror up my spine was so great that it was all I could do to stay still and not let it show. He continued,

"The thrill ... the thrill is like NOTHING else I've ever had, and I've had a lot of thrills.

The only thing that made it sweeter is working in this shit show ... getting lauded as a hero while I built my collection , stacked up my body count.

It really is priceless. No one suspects you, you learn from the best in the business and have access to everything you could need to hone your craft ... it's a serial killer's dream. "

I couldn't help but recall the conversation we'd had, after the Long Island Serial Killer was apprehended. The conversation where I expressed surprise that it wasn't the dirty cop on the case, and he'd suggested that it could have been both because, frequently, bad cops would emulate the killers they were assigned to catch as a way to cover up their own crimes.

I couldn't breathe,

I really did feel nausea now ...

no pretend needed.

Hot tears of disgust and hurt and anger-more than anything anger- started seeping out of my eyes and sliding silently down my cheek. He leaned in and whispered , "What's wrong sweetie? ... don't be sad, I love you ." he said the last bit with mock sincerity and that devious smile I used to think charming , before licking the side of my tear drenched cheek from chin to forehead .

I closed my eyes , and sent up the most earnest silent prayer I've ever said.

But I opened them quickly as I felt the cool metal blade slice shallowly into my cheek, and the warm blood trickle down my neck. I screamed, but the tape deadened all sound .

"Scream all you want - this room is sound proof - and no one will be anywhere near here for hourrrsss ..."

He licked the blood dramatically, slowly, off of my cheek , before reiterating in a whisper , "I've got you for hours."

He unzipped his pants and ripped the duct top off my mouth with his white bony fingers-his skeletal frame eerily silhouetted in the dim light of the distant camera.

"Now let's use those lips while they're still attached eh baby ?" he said, half to me and half to the lens that bore witness to what was rapidly seeming like my untimely and gruesome demise.

For a few brief moments which seemed like hours , I contemplated : "Is this really how it ends?

...

How my story ends??

...

How I end???

-Tortured to death as the subject of some twisted fuck's snuff flick??

How did it come to this?

All I did was try to find love, dare to believe against all logic that I'd finally found it.

Sure, I put up with more than I should have- but I did it out of love, out of empathy, out of hope- however misguided.

I stayed out of trauma from the last dickstain that subjected me to a (in that case metaphorically) gutting horror film irl.

What had I spent my last few years (it would seem on earth), doing?

Was I enjoying life, living it to the fullest?

NO...

I'd been killing myself, risking the exact type of demise that was currently in progress, in order to play the hero.

Was I 'playing' though, really?

And had I 'failed' if I died?

Would it still be worth it?

Was I in over my head?

Should I have just 'left it alone' ?

Should I have been more selfish, perhaps just chosen to ignore blatant evil like the vast majority??"

At the mere internal suggestion of the latter - something in me hardened.

I'm no hero- perhaps- but I sure as fuck was not "playing" anything.

However, if this deranged bastard wanted a "show" , I'd give him a performance worth DYING for.

Before he could grab the knife back off of the table
, I stared up at him with a look of "terror" I knew
he wouldn't be able to resist getting a gander at,
that would distract him just long enough.

Then, moving swiftly towards his open crotch, I
clenched down as hard as I could on his sorry excuse
for an appendage- Bobbitt style, allll the way baby.

He screamed in surprised agony. He was momentarily
thrown off guard, so I ripped my sweaty wrists out
of the duct tape.

His soulless eyes widened as I grabbed the knife from
the tray beside me and thrust it into where I hoped
his femoral artery was.

As he started gushing blood, I guess I must have hit
my mark. I managed to break the rest of the way out
of the chair and bear hugged him just long enough to
grab the gun tucked in his pants. He stumbled back
in shock, and I somehow avoided going into the same-
despite my increasingly blood drenched torso.

Conveniently, and rather poetically, he landed
backwards on the plastic he'd laid for me . He laid
grasping his leg , trying to get the blood to stop.
I briefly considered calling the ambulance; maybe he
could be saved.

I wanted him to stand trial alive for his crimes. I
didn't want to kill anyone .

My hands were shaking violently as I held the gun ,
tears still flooding down my face .

Time stood still for a few moments that seemed like
hours as I thought,

"What is our role in justice? I know self-defense
isn't the same as murder ... but how far does this
sentiment really go? What about the defense of
others, of society ? What about proactive self-
defense ? Defending yourself and your society from
monsters before they have a gun to your head, before
they kill or rape or 'ruin' anyone else ??

Why is it 'justice' if the system does it but
'murder' if we the people take it into our own hands
and can we trust a 'justice' system made up of
'HEROS' like the one I was about to have to kill to
save my own skin? A 'hero' who had wrecked dozens
perhaps hundreds of lives?

Those comic books from my youth never really
addressed THIS scenario; the kill to save YOURSELF
scenarios.

There always seemed to be a hero , a villain and a
victim (or near victim)- in 3 distinct and non-
overlapping roles. You saw hero's kill to save
another person, perhaps, but I don't recall ever
really seeing a hero kill to save themselves.

It's almost as if, from childhood we're brainwashed
into thinking that 'victim' and 'hero' are two
incompatible roles. It's almost as if we've been
taught from youth that we need a big, strong man in
a cape to save us from ... well, usually another big
strong man in a somewhat similar cape.

We are taught that we're incapable of saving
ourselves , furthermore, the implication is that even
if we somehow manage to defy that expectation - we
are certainly no 'hero' for it."

The moment ended, as did my lengthy internal
monologue, and before I knew what was happening he'd
suddenly grabbed the blood soaked plastic where he
laid and jerked it hard enough to make me fall onto
my back off of the plastic a few feet from him.
Disorientated, I started to stumble up, but he was
lurching towards me before I could rise from
crouching.

I looked up at him - as I quickly took hold of the
gun that had fallen ... one more time, I looked at
this creature I thought was the love of my life, my
hero -but all I saw was bloodlust , evil, murder...
a villain masquerading as a hero- then I looked
away, as I pulled the trigger, this time without
any hesitation .

It was a close up shot, and the mess-which ended up
primarily on the wall to our right and back
splattered across my own torso - was one of the most
traumatizing things I've ever experienced.

I laid there shaking, crying , screaming and wishing
against all reason that this was all some kind of
horrible nightmare. I knew undoubtably that I'd done
the right thing. I didn't for a moment regret it,
but that doesn't mean that it didn't tear me apart
to have to do it.

It's not like the movies, real death...

real gore...

real bloodshed.

The putrid smells, the haunting noise of a bullet
entering flesh- it feels intrinsically like nothing
we are ever meant to experience much less enact as
humans. That smell, I don't think you ever erase the
stain of it from your senses. The sounds, the sight,

they cast a ghostly shadow that never fully leaves
you.

Murder, even in self-defense, is horror I wouldn't
wish on anyone.

Finally, I pulled myself together enough to
understand what I had to do next.

So Fresh And So Clean (Clean)

I put on some of his black sterile crime scene gloves
- the ones in his backpack, I wiped the excess blood
from around his body but didn't move him from where
he lay, beside the wall where the shot was fired . I
wiped the area where I had been so there wouldn't be
any shoe marks or outlines of a second person.

I bundled up all the bloody plastic and duct tape
and put it in one of the garbage bags he'd brought.
I got out his phone and started to type out a
suicide note including a confession and the location
of the "films" in his room in the closet... before
realizing there's no way I could make this look like
a suicide-despite how oddly karmatic that would have
been. No, due to the abrasions on his rape-y
appendage and a massive stab wound in his leg, this
would undoubtedly be found to be a murder.

Was it "murder" ??

The reality hit me like a semi in the fast lane.

It was self- defense; I had no choice.

It was kill or be killed, and I chose to live.

I erased the note and left my own simple text, "look
in his childhood closet. He's a killer; I did what I
had to do." I put the phone in his pocket with the
note open. I put the "kill kit" back in his car, and
took my purse, the garbage bag of bloody plastic and
the camera that had been recording us with me. With
one last look back at the nightmare I'd found myself
in, I pulled his hoodie down over my eyes and
"borrowed" his keys to make my escape. The cameras
would just see a hooded figure and his car with

darkly tinted windows drive away. They'd be none the wiser till the next shift change, which gave me maybe 8-10 hours at best to get the fuck out of town. I locked the evidence locker keys inside to buy me a few extra precious minutes.

He'd always told me if I ever found myself committing murder out of necessity - I should go to the cops and explain ... so, naturally, I fully intended to do the opposite.

Why not leave it to the "justice system" to see my innocence, that I acted in self -defense?

Because I believed in justice, but as for the system? Well, thanks to Skeletor (as he'll now be called) I was feeling a wee bit skeptical- plus, I had no way of knowing whether he was the only dirty cop or if there were more of them.

Murder or not- I WAS my own fucking "hero" or perhaps "anti-hero", and now?

It was REALLY time to get out of town.

Scorched Earth

I headed back to our "safe" house, the term suddenly feeling sickeningly ironic.

Something during Skeletor's monologue had stuck out to me, the mention of me digging in his things. The "pregnancy" he obviously found out through some type of spyware or the like on my device, but the box- the only way he could know about that was if he had a camera set up watching me.

If he'd done it in his last place, for a mere two weeks of surveillance while I stayed there- I was uncomfortably confident he would have installed one or more at our "safe house".

I did a rapid sweep of the entire house, and sure enough, the bastard had 2 in the bedroom, 1 in the living area, 1 at each of the exits.

This is what "trust" had awarded me with.

I kept the devices and threw his laptop in my go bag, as I was sure I'd find a treasure trove there too.

I slipped in the contacts I'd already purchased for "our" move- despite my aforementioned (irrational?) fear of putting glass on my eyeballs.

I stared into the mirror, still splatted with my now deceased boyfriend's toothpaste, as I cleaned his blood off my arms. I used nearly an entire bottle of mouth wash. I pushed down the nausea, clasping the cold edges of the porcelain sink to steady myself. Taking out my rather comically oversized scissors, I lopped off my long locks at an angle. Putting on a fresh pair of those black nitrate gloves, I saturated

what was left of my mane in the previously purchased
black dye.

After completing this little impromptu makeover, I
pulled on a dark hoodie, my favorite long sweater,
black tights and my boots. I bagged up all the
garbage and gathered only what I needed for the trip.
Then, I tossed all of it into my car, grabbed both
cats and headed for the interstate- but not before
making one more stop in a back alley way on the
outskirts of Oakland.

Full Circle

And that about catches us up to me in an alley,
madly spray-painting a -formerly jeeringly lime
green- car black and securing a tag from the last
person I can completely trust...

I CAN completely trust, because he's dead.

The running nose? Well, yeah, I'm still human- even
if I had to get rid of someone who wasn't in order
to survive.

I'd ditch the garbage bags in desert a few states
over, as a (perhaps feeble) attempt at slowing down
his buddies in blue from connecting the dots once
they found his body in that evidence locker.

I'd keep the video though ... I'd send it to my
family and friends -with a fervent request they NOT
view but keep - as well as every media outlet possible
as soon as it was safe (er) to do so.

I know I've said a lot about lines- dotted lines,
faded lines, curvy lines, disappearing lines-

but let me make one thing INCREDIBLY clear: there are
some bright glaring, solid, yellow ones in the this
fucked up, crazy world.

In life, much like the on roads we travel, sure you
encounter white dotted lines- where it's ok to weave
in and out and side to side, because you're still
going in the same general direction-

but then there's the double sided yellow lines- the
"do not pass under any circumstances" lines, and for
good reason.

"People" like Skeletor, Fuckface, and the other hypno-rapists who I hunt... they crossed the yellow line, without any concern for who they may have taken out in the process. So, as far as I'm concerned, they don't deserve the title of "people", anymore.

Spyder never did entirely agree with this sentiment. He said it was dehumanizing to call a "man" a "monster". But the thing is, they weren't "men" and they dehumanized themselves by acting like a creature. More importantly, they -momentarily- dehumanized their victims by their depraved cruelty and complete lack of remorse.

To call these creatures who prey on the innocent and unsuspecting "human" would be an insult and a disservice to the rest of us with intact souls.

So these creatures who cross the line, who willfully harm for their own sick entertainment and pleasure , who wreck lives and take them for "fun", they <u>can fucking rot</u>.

Sure it's possible (technically) for them to turn around , to be human again- but it'd require a complete U-turn and frankly , it's just incredibly unlikely.

Regardless, their fate is their choice and their fault.

There aren't many of these double-sided yellow lines, but they exist-

<u>JUST DON'T CROSS THE DAMN YELLOW LINES.</u>

Parting Gifts

If removing one life saves another , is that justice... is that just?

To some extent our "justice" system wis based on this idea ... protecting society from those monsters that just won't stop hurting .

But then again, where's the line? And what the hell are we to do with those who cross it??

Would blind rebel justice descend into anarchy , chaos, presumptive violence??

I'm not speaking of punishment for "accidental" crimes. I'm talking about crimes with intent, intent to harm, to eviscerate, another human for "fun".

Anyone with an intact soul would undoubtedly shudder at this type of offender, would hate them immediately. Does our hatred , our emotion, turn justice to blood lust... to vengeance? I don't know, but I don't think so.

I think "righteous indignation" is a reasonable motivator in seeking and carrying out justice. Maybe it's more about what type of emotion.

In a perfect world, I think we'd execute out of love and not hate.

We'd do what we have to out of love for everyone we're saving in the process, for everyone we were too late to save. I've heard it said a henchman kills out of love for their boss, and that's why they're willing to risk everything... because love is a much more powerful motivator than even the strongest of hate.

The line between love for society, and hate for the perpetrators that torment it?

Well, it's a very thin (probably dotted) line.

So yeah...

That first Fuckface, the guy who tranced me and sent me down this hellish rabbit hole to begin with?

Still no word or sighting of him, go figure.

As for the discord list with trigger words and addresses that had been used for trafficking, somehow they all got very scrambled it seems. And I guess after one or two hypnofucks little trancy tricks didn't work, and after some were even directed to the dwellings of very large angry men instead of the small single women they thought they were surprising in the twilight hours, well the rest of the bunch got too nervous to trust anything on the server.

As for the (presumably?) now departed Fuckface's little ring of rape-y assholes, and Osbourn himself?

Who really knows...

but I heard a rumor that a local biker club was somehow made aware of their younger victims showcased on the dark web ... and I don't think they looked very kindly on that.

I hear someone made these biker clubs aware of those hypnofucks home addresses, phone numbers, appearances, habits etc.

The internet really is such a wonder, isn't it?? - bringing allll types of people together.

Because sometimes, sometimes, I guess maybe what a gal really needs is not only to be her own hero... but also to know a few anti-heroes or anti-villains, those folks who do what hero's won't or maybe just can't.

My last gift to those "friends" I made online, the ones that enjoyed my videos so much? They might have gotten an extra surprise attached upon download with the last full length feature I sent before I skipped town , because viruses deserve viruses ☺

But I digress.

My "faith" in the cops was (I think understandably) at an all time low, and I didn't know who -if anyone - I could trust, but I had to do something with all of that research, all of that info I gathered.

And if you're reading this , then that means my manilla envelopes with my research and last wishes made it to all the right people, and they actually opened that extra flash drive as instructed, and (hopefully) published it as I requested. It means the original file of what happened in that evidence locker, what I had to do to escape the clutches of my lover turned tormentor, has proved my innocence and is in too many hands to contain.

Also, in the envelope, I included a web address hosting an e-version of this little expose , complete with what some might call a doxx list of justice worthy shitbags who are involved with the specific use of NLP and trancing to facilitate rape - complete with addresses, screen shots of actual discord convos , usernames, real names etc etc. We'll see how long that stays up, before one of them takes it out, but I tried anyway.

As for I.C.O.M. , any comprehensive list of members would have ended with my site being taken down in seconds , but I've provided enough information on the USB to spur questions. If enough of us refuse to bury this shit- if we drag it into the light of day and refuse to stop digging - one day I do believe we can bring them down.

Perhaps one at a time... perhaps quietly, before they know what's about to hit them.

So now you know what's happened, where I am (sort of) and how I got here.

This is to be my last book written as -sort of- myself... or at least my last book as the scientific name of a passion flower.

You don't fuck with cults... and you certainly don't fuck with dirty cops or international sadist secret societies with wayyyy too much knowledge on you.

Maybe I decided to enact change in smaller but equally meaningful ways in a more calm environment, perhaps via running away to Europe on a fake passport and starting over. Perhaps I fell in (actual) love there, and got that simple rose garden orgasm life I always dreamed of -

Maybe I decided to stop bitching about "the system" and work from within to improve it. Perhaps via taking my "talents" to an agency who could use them to make positive change with higher clearance levels. And potentially, I added a few lovers who keep me occupied in my limited free time-

Or maybe I stayed a weird little rouge agent of chaotic justice, capitalized on my "gift" for attracting shitbags, became a PI and a bounty hunter and started my own little lady gang with likeminded pissed off boss bitches- who occasionally seek assistance from a sexy anti-hero or even a somewhat questionable anti-villain.

Who knows, and who cares?

Wouldn't they all be a pretty great way to end one crazy adventure and start another?

My closing advice? Don't mistake a villain for a hero , or an anti-villain for a villain , or an anti- hero for a hero.

Maybe just be your own hero (or something between hero and anti-hero), because maybe that's the only kind that exists...

and maybe don't discount the merits of an anti-hero or an anti-villain, regardless of their motivation. I mean, don't ever trust them completely... maybe don't trust anyone completely but yourself,

but recognize that they have their place and their value.

Sometimes maybe you need an anti-something to do things hero's won't or can't, to wipe out the true villains of the world- the worst kind - <u>the kind that masquerade as hero's and attempt to take their atrocities to the grave.</u>

Whether you work to make the system better from the inside, or you work to make the world brighter outside of it ...

whether your influence is small and calm but far
echoing or large and risky in its maneuvering-

no matter how you choose to fight the destroyers, the
most important thing is to never- ever- stop
fighting.

At any rate, regardless, this is (probably) my last
book-

as whoever the fuck I am now,

  And my 1st published work,

      of -

  Probably ?-

    (mostly)

     "fiction".

Completely (*Totally*) Unrelated (But
Interesting) Links:

Oto-usa.org

Darkodyssey.com

Darkdollrebecca.com

Freemanarts.wixsite.com

Mast.net

NLPplanet.org

Post-Hypnotic.com

NLPpower.com

Soj.org

Stevehodel.com

Surrealismtoday.com

wickedgroundsannex.com

*These websites/ organizations in no way
support, condone or are associated with this
publication in any way, shape or form (other
than Post-hypnotic.com as previously stated,
assuming I'm able to keep control of that site
after this publication)